I0570538

Large Print Edition

TWO GHOSTLY MYSTERIES

A Chapter in the History of a Tyrone Family;

&

The Murdered Cousin

SPECIAL LARGE PRINT EDITION
with easy-to-read text

Joseph Sheridan Lefanu

Serenity
Publishers, LLC
ROCKVILLE, MARYLAND
2012

ISBN: 978-1-60450-999-1

NOTE
Serenity Publishers can custom create classic texts in large print
We can create new titles with text/margins to your specifications
Add your notes and create the book as you want it
Combine different classic texts in one volume
Produce an edition with a special introduction or an afterword
Add your footnotes
Visit **www.SerenityPublishers.com** &
www.ArcManor.com
or email **chandi@serenitypublishers.com**

Published by Serenity Publishers
An Arc Manor Company
P. O. Box 10339
Rockville, MD 20849-0339
www.SerenityPublishers.com

Printed in the United States of America/United Kingdom

CONTENTS

A CHAPTER IN THE HISTORY OF A
TYRONE FAMILY

*Being a Tenth Extract from the Legacy of the Late
Francis Purcell, P.P. of Drumcoolagh*

INTRODUCTION

IN the following narrative, I have endeavoured to
give as nearly as possible the "ipsissima verba" of
the valued friend from whom I received it, conscious that any aberration from her mode of telling the tale of her own life, would at once impair
its accuracy and its effect. Would that, with her
words, I could also bring before you her animated
gesture, her expressive countenance, the solemn
and thrilling air and accent with which she related
the dark passages in her strange story; and, above
all, that I could communicate the impressive consciousness that the narrator had seen with her own
eyes, and personally acted in the scenes which she
described; these accompaniments, taken with the

additional circumstance, that she who told the tale was one far too deeply and sadly impressed with religious principle, to misrepresent or fabricate what she repeated as fact, gave to the tale a depth of interest which the events recorded could hardly, themselves, have produced. I became acquainted with the lady from whose lips I heard this narrative, nearly twenty years since, and the story struck my fancy so much, that I committed it to paper while it was still fresh in my mind, and should its perusal afford you entertainment for a listless half hour, my labour shall not have been bestowed in vain. I find that I have taken the story down as she told it, in the first person, and, perhaps, this is as it should be. She began as follows.

My maiden name was Richardson,[1] the designation of a family of some distinction in the county of Tyrone. I was the younger of two daughters, and we were the only children. There was a difference in our ages of nearly six years, so that I did not, in my childhood, enjoy that close companionship

---

1 I have carefully altered the names as they appear in the original MSS., for the reader will see that some of the circumstances recorded are not of a kind to reflect honour upon those involved in them; and, as many are still living, in every way honoured and honourable, who stand in close relation to the principal actors in this drama, the reader will see the necessity of the course which we have adopted.

which sisterhood, in other circumstances, necessarily involves; and while I was still a child, my sister was married. The person upon whom she bestowed her hand, was a Mr. Carew, a gentleman of property and consideration in the north of England. I remember well the eventful day of the wedding; the thronging carriages, the noisy menials, the loud laughter, the merry faces, and the gay dresses. Such sights were then new to me, and harmonized ill with the sorrowful feelings with which I regarded the event which was to separate me, as it turned out, for ever, from a sister whose tenderness alone had hitherto more than supplied all that I wanted in my mother's affection. The day soon arrived which was to remove the happy couple from Ashtown-house. The carriage stood at the hall-door, and my poor sister kissed me again, and again, telling me that I should see her soon. The carriage drove away, and I gazed after it until my eyes filled with tears, and, returning slowly to my chamber, I wept more bitterly, and so, to speak more desolately, than ever I had done before. My father had never seemed to love, or to take an interest in me. He had desired a son, and I think he never thoroughly forgave me my unfortunate sex. My having come into the world at all as his child, he regarded as a kind of fraudulent intrusion, and, as his antipathy to me had its origin in an imperfection of mine, too radical for removal, I never even hoped to stand high in his good graces. My mother was, I dare say, as fond of me as she was of any one; but she was a woman of a masculine and a worldly cast of mind. She had no tenderness or sympathy for the weaknesses, or even for the affections of woman's nature, and her demeanour towards me was peremptory, and often even harsh. It is not to be supposed, then, that I found in the society of my parents much to supply the loss of my sister. About a year after her marriage, we received letters from Mr. Carew, containing accounts of my sister's health, which, though not actually alarming, were calculated to make us seriously uneasy. The symptoms most dwelt upon, were loss of appetite and cough. The letters concluded by intimating that he would avail himself of my father and mother's repeated invitation to spend some time at Ashtown, particularly as the physician who had been consulted as to my sister's health had strongly advised a removal to her native air. There were added repeated assurances that nothing serious was apprehended, as it was supposed that a deranged state of the liver was the only source of the symptoms which seemed to intimate consumption. In accordance with this announcement, my sister and Mr. Carew arrived in Dublin, where one of my father's carriages awaited them, in readiness to start upon whatever day or hour they might choose for their departure. It was arranged that Mr. Carew was, as soon as the day upon which they were to leave Dublin was definitely fixed, to write to my father, who intended that the two last stages should be performed by his own horses, upon whose speed and safety far more reliance might be placed than upon those of the ordinary *post-horses*, which were, at that time, almost without exception, of the very worst order. The journey, one of about ninety miles, was to be divided; the larger portion to be reserved for the second day. On Sunday, a letter reached us, stating that the party would leave Dublin on Monday, and, in due course, reach Ashtown upon Tuesday evening. Tuesday came: the evening closed in, and yet no carriage appeared; darkness came on, and still no sign of our expected visitors. Hour after hour passed away, and it was now past twelve; the night was remarkably calm, scarce a breath stirring, so that any sound, such as that produced by the rapid movement of a vehicle, would have been audible at a considerable distance. For some such sound I was feverishly listening. It was, however, my father's rule to close the house at nightfall, and the window-shutters being fastened, I was unable to reconnoitre the avenue as I would have wished. It was nearly one o'clock, and we began almost to despair of seeing them upon that night, when I thought I distinguished the sound of wheels, but so remote and faint as to make me at first very uncertain. The noise approached; it become louder and clearer; it stopped for a moment. I now heard the shrill screaking of the rusty iron, as the avenue gate revolved on its hinges; again came the sound of wheels in rapid motion.

"It is they," said I, starting up, "the carriage is in the avenue." We all stood for a few moments, breathlessly listening. On thundered the vehicle with the speed of a whirlwind; crack went the whip, and clatter went the wheels, as it rattled over the uneven pavement of the court; a general and furious barking from all the dogs about the house, hailed its arrival. We hurried to the hall in time to hear the steps let down with the sharp clanging noise peculiar to the operation, and the hum of voices exerted in the bustle of arrival. The hall-door was now thrown open, and we all stepped forth to greet our visitors. The court was perfectly empty; the moon was shining broadly and brightly upon all around; nothing was to be seen but the tall trees with their long spectral shadows, now wet with the dews of midnight. We stood gazing from right to left, as if suddenly awakened from a dream; the dogs walked suspiciously, growling and snuffing about the court, and by totally and suddenly ceasing their former loud barking, as also by carrying their tails between their legs, expressing the predominance of fear. We looked one upon the other in perplexity and dismay, and I think I never beheld more pale faces assembled. By my father's direction, we looked about to find anything which might indicate or account for the noise which we had heard; but no such thing was to be seen—even the mire which lay upon the avenue was undisturbed. We returned to the house, more panic struck than I can describe. On the next day, we learned by a messenger, who had ridden hard the greater part of the night, that my sister was dead. On Sunday evening, she had retired to bed rather unwell, and, on Monday, her indisposition declared itself unequivocally to be malignant fever. She became hourly worse, and, on Tuesday night, a little after midnight, she expired.[2] I mention this circumstance, because it

---

2 The residuary legatee of the late Francis Purcell, who has the honour of selecting such of his lamented old friend's manuscripts as may appear fit for publication, in order that the lore which they contain may reach the world before scepticism and utility have robbed our species of the precious gift of credulity, and scornfully kicked before them, or trampled into annihilation, those harmless fragments of picturesque superstition, which it is our object to preserve, has been subjected to the charge of dealing too largely in the marvellous; and it has been half insinuated that such is his love for diablerie, that he is content to wander a mile out of his way, in order to meet a fiend or a goblin, and thus to sacrifice all regard for truth and accuracy to the idle hope of affrighting the imagination, and thus pandering to the bad taste of

was one upon which a thousand wild and fantastical reports were founded, though one would have thought that the truth scarcely required to be improved upon; and again, because it produced a strong and lasting effect upon my spirits, and indeed, I am inclined to think, upon my character. I was, for several years after this occurrence, long after the violence of my grief subsided, so wretchedly low-spirited and nervous, that I could

---

his reader. He begs leave, then, to take this opportunity of asserting his perfect innocence of all the crimes laid to his charge, and to assure his reader that he never pandered to his bad taste, nor went one inch out of his way to introduce witch, fairy, devil, ghost, or any other of the grim fraternity of the redoubted Raw-head and bloody-bones. His province, touching these tales, has been attended with no difficulty and little responsibility; indeed, he is accountable for nothing more than an alteration in the names of persons mentioned therein, when such a step seemed necessary, and for an occasional note, whenever he conceived it possible, innocently, to edge in a word. These tales have been *written down,* as the heading of each announces, by the Rev. Francis Purcell, P.P. of Drumcoolagh; and in all the instances, which are many, in which the present writer has had an opportunity of comparing the manuscript of his departed friend with the actual traditions which are current amongst the families whose fortunes they pretend to illustrate, he has uniformly found that whatever of supernatural occurred in the story, so far from having been exaggerated by him, had been rather softened down, and, wherever it could be attempted, accounted for.

scarcely be said to live, and during this time, habits of indecision, arising out of a listless acquiescence in the will of others, a fear of encountering
even the slightest opposition, and a disposition to
shrink from what are commonly called amuse-
ments, grew upon me so strongly, that I have
scarcely even yet, altogether overcome them. We
saw nothing more of Mr. Carew. He returned to
England as soon as the melancholy rites attendant
upon the event which I have just mentioned were
performed; and not being altogether inconsolable,
he married again within two years; after which,
owing to the remoteness of our relative situations,
and other circumstances, we gradually lost sight
of him. I was now an only child; and, as my elder
sister had died without issue, it was evident that,
in the ordinary course of things, my father's property, which was altogether in his power, would go
to me, and the consequence was, that before I was
fourteen, Ashtown-house was besieged by a host
of suitors; however, whether it was that *I* was too
young, or that none of the aspirants to my hand
stood sufficiently high in rank or wealth, I was
suffered by both parents to do exactly as I pleased;
and well was it for me, as I afterwards found that
fortune, or, rather Providence, had so ordained it,
that I had not suffered my affections to become in
any degree engaged, for my mother would never
have suffered any *silly fancy* of mine, as she was

in the habit of styling an attachment, to stand in the way of her ambitious views; views which she was determined to carry into effect, in defiance of every obstacle, and in order to accomplish which, she would not have hesitated to sacrifice anything so unreasonable and contemptible as a girlish passion.

When I reached the age of sixteen, my mother's plans began to develope themselves, and, at her suggestion, we moved to Dublin to sojourn for the winter, in order that no time might be lost in disposing of me to the best advantage. I had been too long accustomed to consider myself as of no importance whatever, to believe for a moment that I was in reality the cause of all the bustle and preparation which surrounded me, and being thus relieved from the pain which a consciousness of my real situation would have inflicted, I journeyed towards the capital with a feeling of total indifference.

My father's wealth and connection had established him in the best society, and, consequently, upon our arrival in the metropolis, we commanded whatever enjoyment or advantages its gaieties afforded. The tumult and novelty of the scenes in which I was involved did not fail considerably to amuse me, and my mind gradually recovered its tone, which was naturally cheerful. It was almost immediately known and reported that I was an heiress, and of course my attractions were pretty generally acknowledged. Among the many gentlemen whom it was my fortune to please, one, ere long, established himself in my mother's good graces, to the exclusion of all less important aspirants. However, I had not understood, or even remarked his attentions, nor, in the slightest degree, suspected his or my mother's plans respecting me, when I was made aware of them rather abruptly by my mother herself. We had attended a splendid ball, given by Lord M—, at his residence in Stephen's-green, and I was, with the assistance of my waiting-maid, employed in rapidly divesting myself of the rich ornaments which, in profuseness and value, could scarcely have found their equals in any private family in Ireland. I had thrown myself into a lounging chair beside the fire, listless and exhausted, after the fatigues of the evening, when I was aroused from the reverie into which I had fallen, by the sound of footsteps approaching my chamber, and my mother entered.

"Fanny, my dear," said she, in her softest tone. "I wish to say a word or two with you before I go to rest. You are not fatigued, love, I hope?"

"No, no, madam, I thank you," said I, rising at the same time from my seat with the formal respect so little practised now.

"Sit down, my dear," said she, placing herself upon a chair beside me; "I must chat with you for a quarter of an hour or so. Saunders (to the maid), you may leave the room; do not close the room door, but shut that of the lobby."

This precaution against curious ears having been taken as directed, my mother proceeded.

"You have observed, I should suppose, my dearest Fanny; indeed, you *must* have observed, Lord Glenfallen's marked attentions to you?"

"I assure you, madam," I began.

"Well, well, that is all right," interrupted my mother; "of course you must be modest upon the matter; but listen to me for a few moments, my love, and I will prove to your satisfaction that your modesty is quite unnecessary in this case. You have done better than we could have hoped, at least, so very soon. Lord Glenfallen is in love with you. I give you joy of your conquest," and saying this, my mother kissed my forehead.

"In love with me!" I exclaimed, in unfeigned astonishment.

"Yes, in love with you," repeated my mother; "devotedly, distractedly in love with you. Why, my dear, what is there wonderful in it; look in the glass, and look at these," she continued, pointing with a smile to the jewels which I had just removed from my person, and which now lay a glittering heap upon the table.

"May there not," said I, hesitating between confusion and real alarm; "is it not possible that some mistake may be at the bottom of all this?"

"Mistake! dearest; none," said my mother. "None, none in the world; judge for yourself; read this, my love," and she placed in my hand a letter, addressed to herself, the seal of which was broken. I read it through with no small surprise. After some very fine complimentary flourishes upon my beauty and perfections, as, also, upon the antiquity and high reputation of our family, it went on to make a formal proposal of marriage, to be communicated or not to me at present, as my mother should deem expedient; and the letter wound up by a request that the writer might be permitted, upon our return to Ashtown-house, which was soon to take place, as the spring was now tolerably advanced, to visit us for a few days, in case his suit was approved.

"Well, well, my dear," said my mother, impatiently; "do you know who Lord Glenfallen is?"

"I do, madam," said I rather timidly, for I dreaded an altercation with my mother.

"Well, dear, and what frightens you?" continued she; "are you afraid of a title? What has he done to alarm you? he is neither old nor ugly."

I was silent, though I might have said, "He is neither young nor handsome."

"My dear Fanny," continued my mother, "in sober seriousness you have been most fortunate in engaging the affections of a nobleman such as Lord Glenfallen, young and wealthy, with first-rate, yes, acknowledged *first-rate* abilities and of a family whose influence is not exceeded by that of any in Ireland—of course you see the offer in the same light that I do—indeed I think you *must.*"

This was uttered in no very dubious tone. I was so much astonished by the suddenness of the whole communication that I literally did not know what to say.

"You are not in love?" said my mother, turning sharply, and fixing her dark eyes upon me, with severe scrutiny.

"No, madam," said I, promptly; horrified, as what young lady would not have been, at such a query.

"I am glad to hear it," said my mother, dryly. "Once, nearly twenty years ago, a friend of mine consulted me how he should deal with a daughter who had made what they call a love match, beggared herself, and disgraced her family; and I said, without hesitation, take no care of her, but cast her off; such punishment I awarded for an offence committed against the reputation of a family not my own; and what I advised respecting the child of another, with full as small compunction I would *do* with mine. I cannot conceive anything more unreasonable or intolerable than that the fortune and the character of a family should be marred by the idle caprices of a girl."

She spoke this with great severity, and paused as if she expected some observation from me. I, however, said nothing.

"But I need not explain to you, my dear Fanny," she continued, "my views upon this subject; you have always known them well, and I have never yet had reason to believe you likely, voluntarily, to offend me, or to abuse or neglect any of those advantages which reason and duty tell you should be improved—come hither, my dear, kiss me, and do not look so frightened. Well, now, about this letter, you need not answer it yet; of course you must be allowed time to make up your mind; in the mean time I will write to his lordship to give him my permission to visit us at Ashtown—good night, my love."

And thus ended one of the most disagreeable, not to say astounding, conversations I had ever had; it would not be easy to describe exactly what were my feelings towards Lord Glenfallen; whatever might have been my mother's suspicions, my heart was perfectly disengaged; and hitherto, although I had not been made in the slightest degree acquainted with his real views, I had liked him very much, as an agreeable, well informed man, whom I was always glad to meet in society; he had served in the navy in early life, and the polish which his manners received in his after intercourse with courts and cities had not served to obliterate that frankness of *manner* which belongs proverbially to the sailor. Whether this apparent candour went deeper than the outward bearing I was yet to learn; however there was no doubt that as far as I had seen of Lord Glenfallen, he was, though perhaps not so young as might have been desired in a lover, a singularly pleasing man, and whatever feeling unfavourable to him had found its way into my mind, arose altogether from the dread, not an

unreasonable one, that constraint might be practised upon my inclinations. I reflected, however,
that Lord Glenfallen was a wealthy man, and one
highly thought of; and although I could never expect to love him in the romantic sense of the term,
yet I had no doubt but that, all things considered,
I might be more happy with him than I could
hope to be at home. When next I met him it was
with no small embarrassment, his tact and good
breeding, however, soon reassured me, and effectually prevented my awkwardness being remarked
upon; and I had the satisfaction of leaving Dublin for the country with the full conviction that
nobody, not even those most intimate with me,
even suspected the fact of Lord Glenfallen's having made me a formal proposal. This was to me a
very serious subject of self gratulation, for, besides
my instinctive dread of becoming the topic of the
speculations of gossip, I felt that if the situation
which I occupied in relation to him were made
publicly known, I should stand committed in a
manner which would scarcely leave me the power
of retraction. The period at which Lord Glenfall-
en had arranged to visit Ashtown-house was now
fast approaching, and it became my mother's wish
to form me thoroughly to her will, and to obtain
my consent to the proposed marriage before his
arrival, so that all things might proceed smoothly
without apparent opposition or objection upon

my part; whatever objections, therefore, I had entertained were to be subdued; whatever disposition to resistance I had exhibited or had been supposed to feel, were to be completely eradicated before he made his appearance, and my mother addressed herself to the task with a decision and energy against which even the barriers, which her imagination had created, could hardly have stood. If she had, however, expected any determined opposition from me, she was agreeably disappointed; my heart was perfectly free, and all my feelings of liking and preference were in favour of Lord Glenfallen, and I well knew that in case I refused to dispose of myself as I was desired, my mother had alike the power and the will to render my existence as utterly miserable as any, even the most ill-assorted marriage could possibly have done. You will remember, my good friend, that I was very young and very completely under the controul of my parents, both of whom, my mother particularly, were unscrupulously determined in matters of this kind, and willing, when voluntary obedience on the part of those within their power was withheld, to compel a forced acquiescence by an unsparing use of all the engines of the most stern and rigorous domestic discipline. All these combined, not unnaturally, induced me to resolve upon yielding at once, and without useless opposition, to what appeared almost to be my fate. The

appointed time was come, and my now accepted
suitor arrived; he was in high spirits, and, if possible, more entertaining than ever. I was not, however, quite in the mood to enjoy his sprightliness;
but whatever I wanted in gaiety was amply made
up in the triumphant and gracious good humour
of my mother, whose smiles of benevolence and
exultation were showered around as bountifully
as the summer sunshine. I will not weary you
with unnecessary prolixity. Let it suffice to say,
that I was married to Lord Glenfallen with all
the attendant pomp and circumstance of wealth,
rank, and grandeur. According to the usage of the
times, now humanely reformed, the ceremony was
made until long past midnight, the season of wild,
uproarious, and promiscuous feasting and revelry.
Of all this I have a painfully vivid recollection,
and particularly of the little annoyances inflicted
upon me by the dull and coarse jokes of the wits
and wags who abound in all such places, and upon
all such occasions. I was not sorry, when, after a
few days, Lord Glenfallen's carriage appeared at
the door to convey us both from Ashtown; for
any change would have been a relief from the irk-
someness of ceremonial and formality which the
visits received in honour of my newly acquired titles hourly entailed upon me. It was arranged that
we were to proceed to Cahergillagh, one of the
Glenfallen estates, lying, however, in a southern

county, so that a tedious journey (then owing to the impracticability of the roads,) of three days intervened. I set forth with my noble companion, followed by the regrets of some, and by the envy of many, though God knows I little deserved the latter; the three days of travel were now almost spent, when passing the brow of a wild heathy hill, the domain of Cahergillagh opened suddenly upon our view. It formed a striking and a beautiful scene. A lake of considerable extent stretching away towards the west, and reflecting from its broad, smooth waters, the rich glow of the setting sun, was overhung by steep hills, covered by a rich mantle of velvet sward, broken here and there by the grey front of some old rock, and exhibiting on their shelving sides, their slopes and hollows, every variety of light and shade; a thick wood of dwarf oak, birch, and hazel skirted these hills, and clothed the shores of the lake, running out in rich luxuriance upon every promontory, and spreading upward considerably upon the side of the hills.

"There lies the enchanted castle," said Lord Glenfallen, pointing towards a considerable level space intervening between two of the picturesque hills, which rose dimly around the lake. This little plain was chiefly occupied by the same low, wild wood which covered the other parts of the domain; but towards the centre a mass of taller and statelier forest trees stood darkly grouped together, and among them stood an ancient square tower, with many buildings of an humbler character, forming together the manor-house, or, as it was more usually called, the court of Cahergillagh. As we approached the level upon which the mansion stood, the winding road gave us many glimpses of the time-worn castle and its surrounding buildings; and seen as it was through the long vistas of the fine old trees, and with the rich glow of evening upon it, I have seldom beheld an object more picturesquely striking. I was glad to perceive, too, that here and there the blue curling smoke ascended from stacks of chimneys now hidden by the rich, dark ivy, which, in a great measure, covered the building; other indications of comfort made themselves manifest as we approached; and indeed, though the place was evidently one of considerable antiquity, it had nothing whatever of the gloom of decay about it.

"You must not, my love," said Lord Glenfallen, "imagine this place worse than it is. I have no taste for antiquity, at least I should not choose a house to reside in because it is old. Indeed I do not recollect that I was even so romantic as to overcome my aversion to rats and rheumatism, those faithful attendants upon your noble relics of feudalism; and I much prefer a snug, modern, unmysterious bed-room, with well-aired sheets, to the waving tapestry, mildewed cushions, and all the other interesting appliances of romance; however, though I cannot promise you all the discomfort generally pertaining to an old castle, you will find legends and ghostly lore enough to claim your respect; and if old Martha be still to the fore, as I trust she is, you will soon have a supernatural and appropriate anecdote for every closet and corner of the mansion; but here we are—so, without more ado, welcome to Cahergillagh."

We now entered the hall of the castle, and while the domestics were employed in conveying our trunks and other luggage which we had brought with us for immediate use to the apartments which Lord Glenfallen had selected for himself and me, I went with him into a spacious sitting room, wainscoted with finely polished black oak, and hung round with the portraits of various of the worthies of the Glenfallen family. This room looked out upon an extensive level covered with the softest green sward, and irregularly bounded by the wild wood I have before mentioned, through the leafy arcade formed by whose boughs and trunks the level beams of the setting sun were pouring; in the distance, a group of dairy maids were plying their task, which they accompanied throughout with snatches of Irish songs which,

mellowed by the distance, floated not unpleas-
ingly to the ear; and beside them sat or lay, with
all the grave importance of conscious protection,
six or seven large dogs of various kinds; farther
in the distance, and through the cloisters of the
arching wood, two or three ragged urchins were
employed in driving such stray kine as had wandered farther than the rest to join their fellows. As
I looked upon this scene which I have described,
a feeling of tranquillity and happiness came upon
me, which I have never experienced in so strong
a degree; and so strange to me was the sensation
that my eyes filled with tears. Lord Glenfallen
mistook the cause of my emotion, and taking me
kindly and tenderly by the hand he said, "Do not
suppose, my love, that it is my intention to *settle*
here, whenever you desire to leave this, you have
only to let me know your wish and it shall be
complied with, so I must entreat of you not to
suffer any circumstances which I can controul to
give you one moment's uneasiness; but here is old
Martha, you must be introduced to her, one of the
heirlooms of our family."

A hale, good-humoured, erect, old woman was
Martha, and an agreeable contrast to the grim,
decrepit hag, which my fancy had conjured up, as
the depository of all the horrible tales in which I
doubted not this old place was most fruitful. She

welcomed me and her master with a profusion of gratulations, alternately kissing our hands and apologising for the liberty, until at length Lord Glenfallen put an end to this somewhat fatiguing ceremonial, by requesting her to conduct me to my chamber if it were prepared for my reception. I followed Martha up an old-fashioned, oak stair-case into a long, dim passage at the end of which lay the door which communicated with the apartments which had been selected for our use; here the old woman stopped, and respectfully requested me to proceed. I accordingly opened the door and was about to enter, when something like a mass of black tapestry as it appeared disturbed by my sudden approach, fell from above the door, so as completely to screen the aperture; the startling unexpectedness of the occurrence, and the rustling noise which the drapery made in its descent, caused me involuntarily to step two or three paces backwards, I turned, smiling and half ashamed to the old servant, and said, "You see what a coward I am." The woman looked puzzled, and without saying any more, I was about to draw aside the curtain and enter the room, when upon turning to do so, I was surprised to find that nothing whatever interposed to obstruct the passage. I went into the room, followed by the servant woman, and was amazed to find that it, like the one below, was wainscoted, and that nothing like drapery was to be found near the door.

"Where is it," said I; "what has become of it?"

"What does your ladyship wish to know?" said the old woman.

"Where is the black curtain that fell across the door, when I attempted first to come to my chamber," answered I.

"The cross of Christ about us," said the old woman, turning suddenly pale.

"What is the matter, my good friend," said I; "you seem frightened."

"Oh, no, no, your ladyship," said the old woman, endeavouring to conceal her agitation; but in vain, for tottering towards a chair, she sunk into it, looking so deadly pale and horror-struck that I thought every moment she would faint.

"Merciful God, keep us from harm and danger," muttered she at length.

"What can have terrified you so," said I, beginning to fear that she had seen something more than had met my eye, "you appear ill, my poor woman."

"Nothing, nothing, my lady," said she, rising; "I beg your ladyship's pardon for making so bold; may the great God defend us from misfortune."

"Martha," said I, "something *has* frightened you very much, and I insist on knowing what it is; your keeping me in the dark upon the subject will make me much more uneasy than any thing you could tell me; I desire you, therefore, to let me know what agitates you; I command you to tell me."

"Your ladyship said you saw a black curtain falling across the door when you were coming into the room," said the old woman.

"I did," said I; "but though the whole thing appears somewhat strange I cannot see any thing in the matter to agitate you so excessively."

"It's for no good you saw that, my lady," said the crone; "something terrible is coming; it's a sign, my lady—a sign that never fails."

"Explain, explain what you mean, my good woman," said I, in spite of myself, catching more than I could account for, of her superstitious terror.

"Whenever something—something *bad* is going to happen to the Glenfallen family, some one that belongs to them sees a black handkerchief or curtain

just waved or falling before their faces; I saw it myself," continued she, lowering her voice, "when I
was only a little girl, and I'll never forget it; I often
heard of it before, though I never saw it till then,
nor since, praised be God; but I was going into
Lady Jane's room to waken her in the morning;
and sure enough when I got first to the bed and
began to draw the curtain, something dark was
waved across the division, but only for a moment;
and when I saw rightly into the bed, there was she
lying cold and dead, God be merciful to me; so,
my lady, there is small blame to me to be daunted
when any one of the family sees it, for it's many's
the story I heard of it, though I saw it but once."

I was not of a superstitious turn of mind; yet I
could not resist a feeling of awe very nearly allied
to the fear which my companion had so unreserv-
edly expressed; and when you consider my situation, the loneliness, antiquity, and gloom of the
place, you will allow that the weakness was not
without excuse. In spite of old Martha's boding
predictions, however, time flowed on in an unruf-
fled course; one little incident, however, though
trifling in itself, I must relate as it serves to make
what follows more intelligible. Upon the day after
my arrival, Lord Glenfallen of course desired to
make me acquainted with the house and domain;
and accordingly we set forth upon our ramble;

when returning, he became for some time silent and moody, a state so unusual with him as considerably to excite my surprise, I endeavoured by observations and questions to arouse him—but in vain; at length as we approached the house, he said, as if speaking to himself, "'twere madness—madness—madness," repeating the word bitterly—"sure and speedy ruin." There was here a long pause; and at length turning sharply towards me in a tone very unlike that in which he had hitherto addressed me, he said, "Do you think it possible that a woman can keep a secret?"

"I am sure," said I, "that women are very much belied upon the score of talkativeness, and that I may answer your question with the same directness with which you put it; I reply that I *do* think a woman can keep a secret."

"But I do not," said he, drily.

We walked on in silence for a time; I was much astonished at his unwonted abruptness; I had almost said rudeness. After a considerable pause he seemed to recollect himself, and with an effort resuming his sprightly manner, he said, "well, well, the next thing to keeping a secret well is, not to desire to possess one—talkativeness and curiosity generally go together; now I shall make test of you in the first place, respecting the latter of these qualities. I shall be your *Bluebeard*—tush, why do I trifle thus; listen to me, my dear Fanny, I speak now in solemn earnest; what I desire is, intimately, inseparably, connected with your happiness and honour as well as my own; and your compliance with my request will not be difficult; it will impose upon you a very trifling restraint during your sojourn here, which certain events which have occurred since our arrival, have determined me shall not be a long one. You must promise me, upon your sacred honour, that you will visit *only* that part of the castle which can be reached from the front entrance, leaving the back entrance and the part of the building commanded immediately by it, to the menials, as also the small garden whose high wall you see yonder; and never at any time seek to pry or peep into them, nor to open the door which communicates from the front part of the house through the corridor with the back. I do not urge this in jest or in caprice, but from a solemn conviction that danger and misery will be the certain consequences of your not observing what I prescribe. I cannot explain myself further at present—promise me, then, these things as you hope for peace here and for mercy hereafter."

I did make the promise as desired, and he appeared relieved; his manner recovered all its gaiety and elasticity, but the recollection of the strange scene which I have just described dwelt painfully upon my mind. More than a month passed away without any occurrence worth recording; but I was not destined to leave Cahergillagh without further adventure; one day intending to enjoy the pleasant sunshine in a ramble through the woods, I ran up to my room to procure my bonnet and shawl; upon entering the chamber, I was surprised and somewhat startled to find it occupied; beside the fireplace and nearly opposite the door, seated in a large, old-fashioned elbow-chair, was placed the figure of a lady; she appeared to be nearer fifty than forty, and was dressed suitably to her age, in a handsome suit of flowered silk; she had a profusion of trinkets and jewellery about her person, and many rings upon her fingers; but although very rich, her dress was not gaudy or in ill taste; but what was remarkable in the lady was, that although her features were handsome, and upon the whole pleasing, the pupil of each eye was dimmed with the whiteness of cataract, and she was evidently stone blind. I was for some seconds so surprised at this unaccountable apparition, that I could not find words to address her.

"Madam," said I, "there must be some mistake here—this is my bed-chamber."

"Marry come up," said the lady, sharply; "*your* chamber! Where is Lord Glenfallen?"

"He is below, madam," replied I; "and I am convinced he will be not a little surprised to find you here."

"I do not think he will," said she; "with your good leave, talk of what you know something about; tell him I want him; why does the minx dilly dally so?"

In spite of the awe which this grim lady inspired, there was something in her air of confident superiority which, when I considered our relative situations, was not a little irritating.

"Do you know, madam, to whom you speak?" said I.

"I neither know nor care," said she; "but I presume that you are some one about the house, so, again, I desire you, if you wish to continue here, to bring your master hither forthwith."

"I must tell you madam," said I, "that I am Lady Glenfallen."

"What's that?" said the stranger, rapidly.

"I say, madam," I repeated, approaching her, that I might be more distinctly heard, "that I am Lady Glenfallen."

"It's a lie, you trull," cried she, in an accent which made me start, and, at the same time, springing forward, she seized me in her grasp and shook me violently, repeating, "it's a lie, it's a lie," with a rapidity and vehemence which swelled every vein of her face; the violence of her action, and the fury which convulsed her face, effectually terrified me, and disengaging myself from her grasp, I screamed as loud as I could for help; the blind woman continued to pour out a torrent of abuse upon me, foaming at the mouth with rage, and impotently shaking her clenched fists towards me. I heard Lord Glenfallen's step upon the stairs, and I instantly ran out; as I past him I perceived that he was deadly pale, and just caught the words, "I hope that demon has not hurt you?" I made some answer, I forget what, and he entered the chamber, the door of which he locked upon the inside; what passed within I know not; but I heard the voices of the two speakers raised in loud and angry altercation. I thought I heard the shrill accents of the woman repeat the words, "let her look to herself"; but I could not be quite sure. This short sentence, however, was, to my alarmed imagination, pregnant with fearful meaning; the storm at length subsided, though not until after a conference of more than two long hours. Lord Glenfallen then returned, pale and agitated, "That unfortunate woman," said he, "is out of her mind; I dare say she treated you to some of her ravings, but you need not dread any further interruption from her, I have brought her so far to reason. She did not hurt you, I trust."

"No, no," said I; "but she terrified me beyond measure." "Well," said he, "she is likely to behave better for the future, and I dare swear that neither you nor she would desire after what has passed to meet again."

This occurrence, so startling and unpleasant, so involved in mystery, and giving rise to so many painful surmises, afforded me no very agreeable food for rumination. All attempts on my part to arrive at the truth were baffled; Lord Glenfallen evaded all my enquiries, and at length peremptorily forbid any further allusion to the matter. I was thus obliged to rest satisfied with what I had actually seen, and to trust to time to resolve the perplexities in which the whole transaction had involved me. Lord Glenfallen's temper and spirits gradually underwent a complete and most painful change; he became silent and abstracted, his manner to me was abrupt and often harsh, some grievous anxiety seemed ever present to his mind; and under its influence his spirits sunk and his temper became soured. I soon perceived that his gaiety was rather that which the stir and excitement of society produces, than the result of a healthy habit of mind; and every day confirmed me in the opinion, that the considerate good nature which I had so much admired in him was little more than a mere manner; and to my infinite grief and surprise, the gay, kind, open-hearted nobleman who had for months followed and flattered me, was rapidly assuming the form of a gloomy, morose, and singularly selfish man; this was a bitter discovery, and I strove to conceal it from myself as long as I could, but the truth was not to be denied, and I was forced to believe that Lord Glenfallen no longer loved me, and that he was at little pains to conceal the alteration in his sentiments. One morning after breakfast, Lord Glenfallen had been for some time walking silently up and down the room, buried in his moody reflections, when pausing suddenly, and turning towards me, he exclaimed,

"I have it, I have it; we must go abroad and stay there, too, and if that does not answer, why—why we must try some more effectual expedient. Lady Glenfallen, I have become involved in heavy embarrassments; a wife you know must share the fortunes of her husband, for better for worse, but I will waive my right if you prefer remaining here—here at Cahergillagh; for I would not have you seen elsewhere without the state to which your rank entitled you; besides it would break your poor mother's heart," he added, with sneering gravity, "so make up your mind—Cahergillagh or France, I will start if possible in a week, so determine between this and then."

He left the room and in a few moments I saw him ride past the window, followed by a mounted servant; he had directed a domestic to inform me that he should not be back until the next day. I was in very great doubt as to what course of conduct I should pursue, as to accompanying him in the continental tour so suddenly determined upon, I felt that it would be a hazard too great to encounter; for at Cahergillagh I had always the consciousness to sustain me, that if his temper at any time led him into violent or unwarrantable treatment of me, I had a remedy within reach, in the protection and support of my own family, from all useful and effective communication with whom, if once in France, I should be entirely debarred. As to remaining at Cahergillagh in solitude, and for aught I knew, exposed to hidden dangers, it appeared to me scarcely less objectionable than the former proposition; and yet I feared that with one or other I must comply, unless I was prepared to come to an actual breach with Lord Glenfallen; full of these unpleasing doubts and perplexities, I retired to rest. I was wakened, after having slept uneasily for some hours, by some person shaking me rudely by the shoulder; a small lamp burned in my room, and by its light, to my horror and amazement, I discovered that my visitant was the self-same blind, old lady who had so terrified me a few weeks before. I started up in the bed, with a view to ring the bell, and alarm the domestics, but she instantly anticipated me by saying, "Do not be frightened, silly girl; if I had wished to harm you I could have done it while you were sleeping, I need not have wakened you; listen to me, now, attentively and fearlessly; for what I have to say, interests you to the full as much as it does me; tell me, here, in the presence of God, did Lord Glenfallen marry you, *actually marry* you?—speak the truth, woman."

"As surely as I live and speak," I replied, "did Lord Glenfallen marry me in presence of more than a hundred witnesses."

"Well," continued she, "he should have told you *then*, before you married him, that he had a wife living, which wife I am; I feel you tremble—tush! do not be frightened. I do not mean to harm you—mark me now—you are not his wife. When I make my story known you will be so, neither in the eye of God nor of man; you must leave this house upon to-morrow; let the world know that your husband has another wife living; go, you, into retirement, and leave him to justice, which will surely overtake him. If you remain in this house after to-morrow you will reap the bitter fruits of your sin," so saying, she quitted the room, leaving me very little disposed to sleep.

Here was food for my very worst and most terrible suspicions; still there was not enough to remove all doubt. I had no proof of the truth of this woman's statement. Taken by itself there was nothing to induce me to attach weight to it; but when I viewed it in connection with the extraordinary mystery of some of Lord Glenfallen's proceedings, his strange anxiety to exclude me from certain portions of the mansion, doubtless, lest I should encounter this person—the strong influence, nay, command, which she possessed over him, a circumstance clearly established by the very fact of her residing in the very place, where of all others, he should least have desired to find her—her thus acting, and continuing to act in direct contradiction to his wishes; when, I say, I viewed her disclosure in connection with all these circumstances, I could not help feeling that there was at least a fearful verisimilitude in the allegations which she had made. Still I was not satisfied, nor nearly so; young minds have a reluctance almost insurmountable to believing upon any thing short of unquestionable proof, the existence of premeditated guilt in any one whom they have ever trusted; and in support of this feeling I was assured that if the assertion of Lord Glenfallen, which nothing in this woman's manner had led me to disbelieve, were true, namely, that her mind was unsound, the whole fabric of my doubts and fears must fall to the ground. I determined to state to Lord Glenfallen freely and accurately the substance of the communication which I had just heard, and in his words and looks to seek for its proof or refutation; full of these thoughts I remained wakeful and excited all night, every moment fancying that I heard the step, or saw the figure of my recent visitor towards whom I felt a species of horror and dread which I can hardly describe. There was something in her face, though her features had evidently been handsome, and were not, at first sight, unpleasing, which, upon a nearer inspection, seemed to indicate the habitual prevalence and indulgence of evil passions, and a power of expressing mere animal anger, with an intenseness that I have seldom seen equalled, and to which an almost unearthly effect was given by the convulsive quivering of the sightless eyes. You may easily suppose that it was no very pleasing reflection to me to consider, that whenever caprice might induce her to return, I was within the reach of this violent, and, for aught I knew, insane woman, who had, upon that very night, spoken to me in a tone of menace, of which her mere words, divested of the manner and look with which she uttered them, can convey but a faint idea. Will you believe me when I tell you that I was actually afraid to leave my bed in order to secure the door, lest I should again encounter the dreadful object lurking in some corner or peeping from behind the window curtains, so very a child was I in my fears.

The morning came, and with it Lord Glenfallen. I knew not, and indeed I cared not, where he might have been; my thoughts were wholly engrossed by the terrible fears and suspicions which my last night's conference had suggested to me; he was, as usual, gloomy and abstracted, and I feared in no very fitting mood to hear what I had to say with patience, whether the charges were true or false. I was, however, determined not to suffer the opportunity to pass, or Lord Glenfallen to leave the room, until, at all hazards, I had unburdened my mind.

"My Lord," said I, after a long silence, summoning up all my firmness, "my lord, I wish to say a few words to you upon a matter of very great importance, of very deep concernment to you and to me." I fixed my eyes upon him to discern, if possible, whether the announcement caused him any uneasiness, but no symptom of any such feeling was perceptible.

"Well, my dear," said he, "this is, no doubt, a very grave preface, and portends, I have no doubt, something extraordinary—pray let us have it without more ado."

He took a chair, and seated himself nearly opposite to me.

"My lord," said I, "I have seen the person who alarmed me so much a short time since, the blind lady, again, upon last night"; his face, upon which my eyes were fixed, turned pale, he hesitated for a moment, and then said—

"And did you, pray madam, so totally forget or spurn my express command, as to enter that portion of the house from which your promise, I might say, your oath, excluded you—answer me that?" he added, fiercely.

"My lord," said I, "I have neither forgotten your *commands*, since such they were, nor disobeyed them. I was, last night, wakened from my sleep, as I lay in my own chamber, and accosted by the person whom I have mentioned—how she found access to the room I cannot pretend to say."

"Ha! this must be looked to," said he, half reflectively; "and pray," added he, quickly, while in turn he fixed his eyes upon me, "what did this person say, since some comment upon her communication forms, no doubt, the sequel to your preface."

"Your lordship is not mistaken," said I, "her statement was so extraordinary that I could not think of withholding it from you; she told me, my lord, that you had a wife living at the time you married me, and that she was that wife."

Lord Glenfallen became ashy pale, almost livid; he made two or three efforts to clear his voice to speak, but in vain, and turning suddenly from me, he walked to the window; the horror and dismay, which, in the olden time, overwhelmed the woman of Endor, when her spells unexpectedly conjured the dead into her presence, were but types of what I felt, when thus presented with what appeared to be almost unequivocal evidence of the guilt, whose existence I had before so strongly doubted. There was a silence of some moments, during which it were hard to conjecture whether I or my companion suffered most. Lord Glenfallen soon recovered his self command; he returned to the table, again sat down and said—

"What you have told me has so astonished me, has unfolded such a tissue of motiveless guilt, and in a quarter from which I had so little reason to look for ingratitude or treachery, that your announcement almost deprived me of speech; the person in question, however, has one excuse, her mind is, as I told you before, unsettled. You should have remembered that, and hesitated to receive as unexceptionable evidence against the honour of your husband, the ravings of a lunatic. I now tell you that this is the last time I shall speak to you upon this subject, and, in the presence of the God who is to judge me, and as I hope for mercy in the day of judgment, I swear that the charge thus brought against me, is utterly false, unfounded, and ridiculous; I defy the world in any point to taint my honour; and, as I have never taken the opinion of madmen touching your character or morals, I think it but fair to require that you will evince a like tenderness for me; and now, once for all, never again dare to repeat to me your insulting suspicions, or the clumsy and infamous calumnies of fools. I shall instantly let the worthy lady who contrived this somewhat original device, understand fully my opinion upon the matter— good morning"; and with these words he left me again in doubt, and involved in all horrors of the most agonizing suspense. I had reason to think that Lord Glenfallen wreaked his vengeance upon the author of the strange story which I had heard, with a violence which was not satisfied with mere words, for old Martha, with whom I was a great favourite, while attending me in my room, told me that she feared her master had ill used the poor, blind, Dutch woman, for that she had heard her scream as if the very life were leaving her, but added a request that I should not speak of what she had told me to any one, particularly to the master.

"How do you know that she is a Dutch woman?" inquired I, anxious to learn anything whatever that might throw a light upon the history of this person, who seemed to have resolved to mix herself up in my fortunes.

"Why, my lady," answered Martha, "the master often calls her the Dutch hag, and other names you would not like to hear, and I am sure she is neither English nor Irish; for, whenever they talk together, they speak some queer foreign lingo, and fast enough, I'll be bound; but I ought not to talk about her at all; it might be as much as my place is worth to mention her—only you saw her first yourself, so there can be no great harm in speaking of her now."

"How long has this lady been here?" continued I.

"She came early on the morning after your lady-ship's arrival," answered she; "but do not ask me any more, for the master would think nothing of turning me out of doors for daring to speak of her at all, much less to *you*, my lady."

I did not like to press the poor woman further; for her reluctance to speak on this topic was evident and strong. You will readily believe that upon the very slight grounds which my information afforded, contradicted as it was by the solemn oath of my husband, and derived from what was, at best, a very questionable source, I could not take any very decisive measure whatever; and as to the menace of the strange woman who had thus unaccountably twice intruded herself into my chamber, although, at the moment, it occasioned me some uneasiness, it was not, even in my eyes, sufficiently formidable to induce my departure from Cahergillagh.

A few nights after the scene which I have just mentioned, Lord Glenfallen having, as usual, early retired to his study, I was left alone in the parlour to amuse myself as best I might. It was not strange that my thoughts should often recur to the agitating scenes in which I had recently taken a part; the subject of my reflections, the solitude, the silence, and the lateness of the hour, as also the depression of spirits to which I had of late been a constant prey, tended to produce that nervous excitement which places us wholly at the mercy of the imagination. In order to calm my spirits, I was endeavouring to direct my thoughts into some more pleasing channel, when I heard, or thought I heard, uttered, within a few yards of me, in an odd half-sneering tone, the words, "There is blood upon your ladyship's throat." So vivid was the impression, that I started to my feet, and involuntarily placed my hand upon my neck. I looked around the room for the speaker, but in vain. I went then to the room-door, which I opened, and peered into the passage, nearly faint with horror, lest some leering, shapeless thing should greet me upon the threshold. When I had gazed long enough to assure myself that no strange object was within sight.

"I have been too much of a rake, lately; I am racking out my nerves," said I, speaking aloud, with a view to reassure myself. I rang the bell, and, attended by old Martha, I retired to settle for the night. While the servant was, as was her custom, arranging the lamp which I have already stated always burned during the night in my chamber, I was employed in undressing, and, in doing so,

I had recourse to a large looking-glass which occupied a considerable portion of the wall in which it was fixed, rising from the ground to a height of about six feet; this mirror filled the space of a large pannel in the wainscoting opposite the foot of the bed. I had hardly been before it for the lapse of a minute, when something like a black pall was slowly waved between me and it.

"Oh, God! there it is," I exclaimed wildly. "I have seen it again, Martha—the black cloth."

"God be merciful to us, then!" answered she, tremulously crossing herself. "Some misfortune is over us."

"No, no, Martha," said I, almost instantly recovering my collectedness; for, although of a nervous temperament, I had never been superstitious. "I do not believe in omens. You know, I saw, or fancied I saw, this thing before, and nothing followed."

"The Dutch lady came the next morning," replied she.

"Methinks, such an occurrence scarcely deserved a supernatural announcement," I replied.

"She is a strange woman, my lady," said Martha, "and she is not *gone* yet—mark my words."

"Well, well, Martha," said I, "I have not wit enough to change your opinions, nor inclination to alter mine; so I will talk no more of the matter. Good night," and so I was left to my reflections. After lying for about an hour awake, I at length fell into a kind of doze; but my imagination was still busy, for I was startled from this unrefreshing sleep by fancying that I heard a voice close to my face exclaim as before, "There is blood upon your ladyship's throat." The words were instantly followed by a loud burst of laughter. Quaking with horror, I awakened, and heard my husband enter the room. Even this was a relief. Scared as I was, however, by the tricks which my imagination had played me, I preferred remaining silent, and pretending to sleep, to attempting to engage my husband in conversation, for I well knew that his mood was such, that his words would not, in all probability, convey anything that had not better be unsaid and unheard. Lord Glenfallen went into his dressing-room, which lay upon the right-hand side of the bed. The door lying open, I could see him by himself, at full length upon a sofa, and, in about half an hour, I became aware, by his deep and regularly drawn respiration, that he was fast asleep. When slumber refuses to visit one, there is something peculiarly irritating, not to the temper, but to the nerves, in the consciousness that some one is in your immediate presence, actually enjoying the boon which you are seeking in vain; at least, I have always found it so, and never more than upon the present occasion. A thousand annoying imaginations harassed and excited me, every object which I looked upon, though ever so familiar, seemed to have acquired a strange phantom-like character, the varying shadows thrown by the flickering of the lamp-light, seemed shaping themselves into grotesque and unearthly forms, and whenever my eyes wandered to the sleeping figure of my husband, his features appeared to undergo the strangest and most demoniacal contortions. Hour after hour was told by the old clock, and each succeeding one found me, if possible, less inclined to sleep than its predecessor. It was now considerably past three; my eyes, in their involuntary wanderings, happened to alight upon the large mirror which was, as I have said, fixed in the wall opposite the foot of the bed. A view of it was commanded from where I lay, through the curtains, as I gazed fixedly upon it, I thought I perceived the broad sheet of glass shifting its position in relation to the bed; I rivetted my eyes upon it with intense scrutiny; it was no deception, the mirror, as if acting of its own impulse moved slowly aside, and disclosed a dark aperture in the wall, nearly as large as an ordinary door; a figure evidently stood in this; but the light was too dim to define it accurately. It stepped cautiously into

the chamber, and with so little noise, that had I
not actually seen it, I do not think I should have
been aware of its presence. It was arrayed in a kind
of woollen night-dress, and a white handkerchief
or cloth was bound tightly about the head; I had
no difficulty spite of the strangeness of the at-
tire in recognising the blind woman whom I so
much dreaded. She stooped down, bringing her
head nearly to the ground, and in that attitude
she remained motionless for some moments, no
doubt in order to ascertain if any suspicious sound
were stirring. She was apparently satisfied by her
observations, for she immediately recommenced
her silent progress towards a ponderous mahog-
any dressing table of my husband's; when she
had reached it, she paused again, and appeared
to listen attentively for some minutes; she then
noiselessly opened one of the drawers from which,
having groped for some time, she took something
which I soon perceived to be a case of razors; she
opened it and tried the edge of each of the two instruments upon the skin of her hand; she quickly
selected one, which she fixed firmly in her grasp;
she now stooped down as before, and having listened for a time, she, with the hand that was disengaged, groped her way into the dressing room
where Lord Glenfallen lay fast asleep. I was fixed
as if in the tremendous spell of a night mare. I
could not stir even a finger; I could not lift my

voice; I could not even breathe, and though I expected every moment to see the sleeping man murdered, I could not even close my eyes to shut out the horrible spectacle, which I had not the power to avert. I saw the woman approach the sleeping figure, she laid the unoccupied hand lightly along his clothes, and having thus ascertained his identity, she, after a brief interval, turned back and again entered my chamber; here she bent down again to listen. I had now not a doubt but that the razor was intended for my throat; yet the terrific fascination which had locked all my powers so long, still continued to bind me fast. I felt that my life depended upon the slightest ordinary exertion, and yet I could not stir one joint from the position in which I lay, nor even make noise enough to waken Lord Glenfallen. The murderous woman now, with long, silent steps, approached the bed; my very heart seemed turning to ice; her left hand, that which was disengaged, was upon the pillow; she gradually slid it forward towards my head, and in an instant, with the speed of lightning, it was clutched in my hair, while, with the other hand, she dashed the razor at my throat. A slight inaccuracy saved me from instant death; the blow fell short, the point of the razor grazing my throat; in a moment I know not how, I found myself at the other side of the bed uttering shriek after shriek; the wretch was, however, determined if possible to murder me; scrambling along by the curtains, she rushed round the bed towards me; I seized the handle of the door to make my escape; it was, however, fastened; at all events I could not open it, from the mere instinct of recoiling terror, I shrunk back into a corner—she was now within a yard of me—her hand was upon my face—I closed my eyes fast, expecting never to open them again, when a blow, inflicted from behind by a strong arm, stretched the monster senseless at my feet; at the same moment the door opened, and several domestics, alarmed by my cries, entered the apartment. I do not recollect what followed, for I fainted. One swoon succeeded another so long and death-like, that my life was considered very doubtful. At about ten o'clock, however, I sunk into a deep and refreshing sleep, from which I was awakened at about two, that I might swear my deposition before a magistrate, who attended for that purpose. I, accordingly, did so, as did also Lord Glenfallen; and the woman was fully committed to stand her trial at the ensuing assizes. I shall never forget the scene which the examination of the blind woman and of the other parties afforded. She was brought into the room in the custody of two servants; she wore a kind of flannel wrapper which had not been changed since the night before; it was torn and soiled, and here and there smeared with blood, which had flowed in large quantities from a wound in her head; the white handkerchief had fallen off in the scuffle; and her grizzled hair fell in masses about her wild and deadly pale countenance. She appeared perfectly composed, however, and the only regret she expressed throughout, was at not having succeeded in her attempt, the object of which she did not pretend to conceal. On being asked her name, she called herself the Countess Glenfallen, and refused to give any other title.

"The woman's name is Flora Van-Kemp," said Lord Glenfallen.

"It *was*, it *was*, you perjured traitor and cheat," screamed the woman; and then there followed a volley of words in some foreign language. "Is there a magistrate here?" she resumed; "I am Lord Glenfallen's wife—I'll prove it—write down my words. I am willing to be hanged or burned, so *he* meets his deserts. I did try to kill that doll of his; but it was he who put it into my head to do it—two wives were too many—I was to murder her, or she was to hang me—listen to all I have to say."

Here Lord Glenfallen interrupted.

"I think, sir," said he, addressing the magistrate, "that we had better proceed to business, this unhappy woman's furious recriminations but waste our time; if she refuses to answer your questions, you had better, I presume, take my depositions."

"And are you going to swear away my life, you black perjured murderer?" shrieked the woman. "Sir, sir, sir, you must hear me," she continued, addressing the magistrate, "I can convict him—he bid me murder that girl, and then when I failed, he came behind me, and struck me down, and now he wants to swear away my life—take down all I say."

"If it is your intention," said the magistrate, "to confess the crime with which you stand charged, you may, upon producing sufficient evidence, criminate whom you please."

"Evidence!—I have no evidence but myself," said the woman. "I will swear it all—write down my testimony—write it down, I say—we shall hang side by side, my brave Lord—all your own handy—work, my gentle husband." This was followed by a low, insolent, and sneering laugh, which, from one in her situation, was sufficiently horrible.

"I will not at present hear anything," replied he, "but distinct answers to the questions which I shall put to you upon this matter."

"Then you shall hear nothing," replied she sullenly, and no inducement or intimidation could bring her to speak again.

Lord Glenfallen's deposition and mine were then given, as also those of the servants who had entered the room at the moment of my rescue; the magistrate then intimated that she was committed, and must proceed directly to gaol, whither she was brought in a carriage of Lord Glenfallen's, for his lordship was naturally by no means indifferent to the effect which her vehement accusations against himself might produce, if uttered before every chance hearer whom she might meet with between Cahergillagh and the place of confinement whither she was dispatched.

During the time which intervened between the committal and the trial of the prisoner, Lord Glenfallen seemed to suffer agonies of mind which baffle all description, he hardly ever slept, and when he did, his slumbers seemed but the instruments of new tortures, and his waking hours were, if possible, exceeded in intensity of terrors by the dreams which disturbed his sleep. Lord Glenfallen rested, if to lie in the mere attitude of repose were to do so, in his dressing-room, and thus I had an opportunity of witnessing, far oftener than I wished it, the fearful workings of his mind; his agony often broke out into such fearful paroxysms that delirium and total loss of reason appeared to be impending; he frequently spoke of flying from the country, and bringing with him all the witnesses of the appalling scene upon which the prosecution was founded; then again he would fiercely lament that the blow which he had inflicted had not ended all.

The assizes arrived, however, and upon the day appointed, Lord Glenfallen and I attended in order to give our evidence. The cause was called on, and the prisoner appeared at the bar. Great curiosity and interest were felt respecting the trial, so that the court was crowded to excess. The prisoner, however, without appearing to take the trouble of listening to the indictment, pleaded guilty, and no representations on the part of the court availed to induce her to retract her plea. After much time had been wasted in a fruitless attempt to prevail upon her to reconsider her words, the court proceeded according to the usual form, to pass sentence. This having been done, the prisoner was about to be removed, when she said in a low, distinct voice—

"A word—a word, my Lord:—is Lord Glenfallen here in the court?" On being told that he was, she raised her voice to a tone of loud menace, and continued—

"Hardress, Earl of Glenfallen, I accuse you here in this court of justice of two crimes—first, that you married a second wife, while the first was living, and again, that you prompted me to the murder, for attempting which I am to die—secure him—chain him—bring him here."

There was a laugh through the court at these words, which were naturally treated by the judge as a violent extemporary recrimination, and the woman was desired to be silent.

"You won't take him, then," she said, "you won't try him? You'll let him go free?"

It was intimated by the court that he would certainly be allowed "to go free," and she was ordered again to be removed. Before, however, the mandate was executed, she threw her arms wildly into the air, and uttered one piercing shriek so full of preternatural rage and despair, that it might fitly have ushered a soul into those realms where hope can come no more. The sound still rang in my ears, months after the voice that had uttered it was for ever silent. The wretched woman was executed in accordance with the sentence which had been pronounced.

For some time after this event, Lord Glenfallen appeared, if possible, to suffer more than he had done before, and altogether, his language, which often amounted to half confessions of the guilt imputed to him, and all the circumstances connected with the late occurrences, formed a mass of evidence so convincing that I wrote to my father, detailing the grounds of my fears, and imploring him to come to Cahergillagh without delay, in order to remove me from my husband's control, previously to taking legal steps for a final separation. Circumstanced as I was, my existence was little short of intolerable, for, besides the fearful suspicions which attached to my husband, I plainly perceived that if Lord Glenfallen were not relieved, and that speedily, insanity must supervene. I therefore expected my father's arrival, or at least a letter to announce it, with indescribable impatience.

About a week after the execution had taken place, Lord Glenfallen one morning met me with an unusually sprightly air—

"Fanny," said he, "I have it now for the first time, in my power to explain to your satisfaction every thing which has hitherto appeared suspicious or mysterious in my conduct. After breakfast come with me to my study, and I shall, I hope, make all things clear."

This invitation afforded me more real pleasure than I had experienced for months; something had certainly occurred to tranquillize my husband's mind, in no ordinary degree, and I thought it by no means impossible that he would, in the proposed interview, prove himself the most injured and innocent of men. Full of this hope I repaired to his study at the appointed hour; he was writing busily when I entered the room, and just raising his eyes, he requested me to be seated. I took a chair as he desired, and remained silently awaiting his leisure, while he finished, folded, directed, and sealed his letter; laying it then upon the table, with the address downward, he said—

"My dearest Fanny, I know I must have appeared very strange to you and very unkind—often even cruel; before the end of this week I will show you the necessity of my conduct; how impossible it was that I should have seemed otherwise. I am conscious that many acts of mine must have inevitably given rise to painful suspicions—suspicions, which indeed, upon one occasion you very properly communicated to me. I have gotten two letters from a quarter which commands respect, containing information as to the course by which I may be enabled to prove the negative of all the crimes which even the most credulous suspicion could lay to my charge. I expected a third by this morning's post, containing documents which will set the matter for ever at rest, but owing, no doubt, to some neglect, or, perhaps, to some difficulty in collecting the papers, some inevitable delay, it has not come to hand this morning, according to my expectation. I was finishing one to the very same quarter when you came in, and if a sound rousing be worth anything, I think I shall have a special messenger before two days have passed. I have been thinking over the matter within myself, whether I had better imperfectly clear up your doubts by submitting to your inspection the two letters which I have already received, or wait till I can triumphantly vindicate myself by the pro-duction of the documents which I have already mentioned, and I have, I think, not unnaturally decided upon the latter course; however, there is a person in the next room, whose testimony is not without its value—excuse me for one moment."

So saying, he arose and went to the door of a closet which opened from the study, this he un-locked, and half opening the door, he said, "It is only I," and then slipped into the room, and carefully closed and locked the door behind him. I immediately heard his voice in animat-ed conversation; my curiosity upon the subject of the letter was naturally great, so smothering any little scruples which I might have felt, I re-solved to look at the address of the letter which lay as my husband had left it, with its face upon the table. I accordingly drew it over to me, and turned up the direction. For two or three moments I could scarce believe my eyes, but there could be no mistake—in large characters were traced the words, "To the Archangel Gabriel in heaven." I had scarcely returned the letter to its original position, and in some degree recovered the shock which this unequivocal proof of insanity produced, when the closet door was unlocked, and Lord Glenfallen re-entered the study, carefully closing and locking the door again upon the outside.

"Whom have you there?" inquired I, making a strong effort to appear calm.

"Perhaps," said he musingly, "you might have some objection to seeing her, at least for a time."

"Who is it?" repeated I.

"Why," said he, "I see no use in hiding it—the blind Dutchwoman; I have been with her the whole morning. She is very anxious to get out of that closet, but you know she is odd, she is scarcely to be trusted."

A heavy gust of wind shook the door at this moment with a sound as if something more substantial were pushing against it.

"Ha, ha, ha!—do you hear her," said he, with an obstreperous burst of laughter. The wind died away in a long howl, and Lord Glenfallen, suddenly checking his merriment, shrugged his shoulders, and muttered—

"Poor devil, she has been hardly used."

"We had better not tease her at present with questions," said I, in as unconcerned a tone as I could assume, although I felt every moment as if I should faint.

"Humph! may be so," said he, "well, come back in an hour or two, or when you please, and you will find us here."

He again unlocked the door, and entered with the same precautions which he had adopted before, locking the door upon the inside, and as I hurried from the room, I heard his voice again exerted as if in eager parley. I can hardly describe my emotions; my hopes had been raised to the highest, and now in an instant, all was gone—the dreadful consummation was accomplished—the fearful retribution had fallen upon the guilty man—the mind was destroyed—the power to repent was gone. The agony of the hours which followed what I would still call my *awful* interview with Lord Glenfallen, I cannot describe; my solitude was, however, broken in upon by Martha, who came to inform me of the arrival of a gentleman, who expected me in the parlour. I accordingly descended, and to my great joy, found my father seated by the fire. This expedition, upon his part, was easily accounted for: my communications had touched the honour of the family. I speedily informed him of the dreadful malady which had fallen upon the wretched man. My father suggested the necessity of placing some person to watch him, to prevent his injuring himself or others. I rang the bell, and desired that one Edward Cooke, an attached servant of the family, should be sent to me. I told him distinctly and briefly, the nature of the service required of him, and, attended by him, my father and I proceeded at once to the study; the door of the inner room was still closed, and everything in the outer chamber remained in the same order in which I had left it. We then advanced to the closet door, at which we knocked, but without receiving any answer. We next tried to open the door, but in vain—it was locked upon the inside; we knocked more loudly, but in vain. Seriously alarmed, I desired the servant to force the door, which was, after several violent efforts, accomplished, and we entered the closet. Lord Glenfallen was lying on his face upon a sofa.

"Hush," said I, "he is asleep"; we paused for a moment.

"He is too still for that," said my father; we all of us felt a strong reluctance to approach the figure.

"Edward," said I, "try whether your master sleeps."

The servant approached the sofa where Lord Glenfallen lay; he leant his ear towards the head of the recumbent figure, to ascertain whether the sound of breathing was audible; he turned towards us, and said—

"My lady, you had better not wait here, I am sure he is dead!"

"Let me see the face," said I, terribly agitated, "you *may* be mistaken."

The man then, in obedience to my command, turned the body round, and, gracious God! what a sight met my view—he was, indeed, perfectly dead. The whole breast of the shirt, with its lace frill, was drenched with gore, as was the couch underneath the spot where he lay. The head hung back, as it seemed almost severed from the body by a frightful gash, which yawned across the throat. The instrument which had inflicted it, was found under his body. All, then, was over; I was never to learn the history in whose termination I had been so deeply and so tragically involved.

The severe discipline which my mind had undergone was not bestowed in vain. I directed my thoughts and my hopes to that place where there is no more sin, nor danger, nor sorrow.

Thus ends a brief tale, whose prominent incidents many will recognize as having marked the history of a distinguished family, and though it refers to a somewhat distant date, we shall be found not to have taken, upon that account, any liberties with the facts, but in our statement of all the incidents, to have rigorously and faithfully adhered to the truth.

THE MURDERED COUSIN

"And they lay wait for their own blood: they lurk privily for their own lives.

"So are the ways of every one that is greedy of gain; which taketh away the life of the owner thereof."

This story of the Irish peerage is written, as nearly as possible, in the very words in which it was related by its "heroine," the late Countess D—, and is therefore told in the first person.

My mother died when I was an infant, and of her I have no recollection, even the faintest. By her death my education was left solely to the direction of my surviving parent. He entered upon his task with a stern appreciation of the responsibility thus cast upon him. My religious instruction was prosecuted with an almost exaggerated anxiety;

and I had, of course, the best masters to perfect me in all those accomplishments which my station and wealth might seem to require. My father was what is called an oddity, and his treatment of me, though uniformly kind, was governed less by affection and tenderness, than by a high and unbending sense of duty. Indeed I seldom saw or spoke to him except at meal-times, and then, though gentle, he was usually reserved and gloomy. His leisure hours, which were many, were passed either in his study or in solitary walks; in short, he seemed to take no further interest in my happiness or improvement, than a conscientious regard to the discharge of his own duty would seem to impose.

Shortly before my birth an event occurred which had contributed much to induce and to confirm my father's unsocial habits; it was the fact that a suspicion of *murder* had fallen upon his younger brother, though not sufficiently definite to lead to any public proceedings, yet strong enough to ruin him in public opinion. This disgraceful and dreadful doubt cast upon the family name, my father felt deeply and bitterly, and not the less so that he himself was thoroughly convinced of his brother's innocence. The sincerity and strength of this conviction he shortly afterwards proved in a manner which produced the catastrophe of my story.

Before, however, I enter upon my immediate adventures, I ought to relate the circumstances which had awakened that suspicion to which I have referred, inasmuch as they are in themselves somewhat curious, and in their effects most intimately connected with my own after-history.

My uncle, Sir Arthur Tyrrell, was a gay and extravagant man, and, among other vices, was ruinously addicted to gaming. This unfortunate propensity, even after his fortune had suffered so severely as to render retrenchment imperative, nevertheless continued to engross him, nearly to the exclusion of every other pursuit. He was, however, a proud, or rather a vain man, and could not bear to make the diminution of his income a matter of triumph to those with whom he had hitherto competed; and the consequence was, that he frequented no longer the expensive haunts of his dissipation, and retired from the gay world, leaving his coterie to discover his reasons as best they might. He did not, however, forego his favourite vice, for though he could not worship his great divinity in those costly temples where he was formerly wont to take his place, yet he found it very possible to bring about him a sufficient number of the votaries of chance to answer all his ends. The consequence was, that Carrickleigh, which was the name of my uncle's residence, was never without one or more of such visiters as I have described. It happened that upon one occasion he was visited by one Hugh Tisdall, a gentleman of loose, and, indeed, low habits, but of considerable wealth, and who had, in early youth, travelled with my uncle upon the Continent. The period of this visit was winter, and, consequently, the house was nearly deserted excepting by its ordinary inmates; it was, therefore, highly acceptable, particularly as my uncle was aware that his visiter's tastes accorded exactly with his own.

Both parties seemed determined to avail themselves of their mutual suitability during the brief stay which Mr. Tisdall had promised; the consequence was, that they shut themselves up in Sir Arthur's private room for nearly all the day and the greater part of the night, during the space of almost a week, at the end of which the servant having one morning, as usual, knocked at Mr. Tisdall's bed-room door repeatedly, received no answer, and, upon attempting to enter, found that it was locked. This appeared suspicious, and the inmates of the house having been alarmed, the door was forced open, and, on proceeding to the bed, they found the body of its occupant perfectly lifeless, and hanging halfway out, the head downwards, and near the floor. One deep wound had been inflicted upon the temple, apparently with some blunt instrument, which had penetrated the brain, and another blow, less effective—probably the first aimed—had grazed his head, removing some of the scalp. The door had been double locked upon the *inside*, in evidence of which the key still lay where it had been placed in the lock. The window, though not secured on the interior, was closed; a circumstance not a little puzzling, as it afforded the only other mode of escape from the room. It looked out, too, upon a kind of court-yard, round which the old buildings stood, formerly accessible by a narrow doorway and passage lying in the oldest side of the quadrangle, but which had since been built up, so as to preclude all ingress or egress; the room was also upon the second story, and the height of the window considerable; in addition to all which the stone window-sill was much too narrow to allow of any one's standing upon it when the window was closed. Near the bed were found a pair of razors belonging to the murdered man, one of them upon the ground, and both of them open. The weapon which inflicted the mortal wound was not to be found in the room, nor were any footsteps or other traces of the murderer discoverable. At the suggestion of Sir Arthur himself, the coroner was instantly summoned to attend, and an inquest was held. Nothing, however, in any degree conclusive was elicited. The walls, ceiling, and floor of the room were carefully examined, in order to ascertain whether they contained a trap-door or other concealed mode of entrance, but no such thing appeared. Such was the minuteness of investigation employed, that, although the grate had contained a large fire during the night, they proceeded to examine even the very chimney, in order to discover whether escape by it were possible. But this attempt, too, was fruitless, for the chimney, built in the old fashion, rose in a perfectly perpendicular line from the hearth, to a height of nearly fourteen feet above the roof, affording in its interior scarcely the possibility of ascent, the flue being smoothly plastered, and sloping towards the top like an inverted funnel; promising, too, even if the summit were attained, owing to its great height, but a precarious descent upon the sharp and steep-ridged roof; the ashes, too, which lay in the grate, and the soot, as far as it could be seen, were undisturbed, a circumstance almost conclusive upon the point.

Sir Arthur was of course examined. His evidence was given with clearness and unreserve, which seemed calculated to silence all suspicion. He stated that, up to the day and night immediately preceding the catastrophe, he had lost to a heavy amount, but that, at their last sitting, he had not only won back his original loss, but upwards of

L4,000 in addition; in evidence of which he produced an acknowledgment of debt to that amount in the handwriting of the deceased, bearing date the night of the catastrophe. He had mentioned the circumstance to Lady Tyrrell, and in presence of some of his domestics; which statement was supported by *their* respective evidence. One of the jury shrewdly observed, that the circumstance of Mr. Tisdall's having sustained so heavy a loss might have suggested to some ill-minded persons, accidentally hearing it, the plan of robbing him, after having murdered him in such a manner as might make it appear that he had committed suicide; a supposition which was strongly supported by the razors having been found thus displaced and removed from their case. Two persons had probably been engaged in the attempt, one watching by the sleeping man, and ready to strike him in case of his awakening suddenly, while the other was procuring the razors and employed in inflicting the fatal gash, so as to make it appear to have been the act of the murdered man himself. It was said that while the juror was making this suggestion Sir Arthur changed colour. There was nothing, however, like legal evidence to implicate him, and the consequence was that the verdict was found against a person or persons unknown, and for some time the matter was suffered to rest, until, after about five months, my father received a letter from a person signing himself Andrew Collis, and representing himself to be the cousin of the deceased. This letter stated that his brother, Sir Arthur, was likely to incur not merely suspicion but personal risk, unless he could account for certain circumstances connected with the recent murder, and contained a copy of a letter written by the deceased, and dated the very day upon the night of which the murder had been perpetrated. Tisdall's letter contained, among a great deal of other matter, the passages which follow:—

"I have had sharp work with Sir Arthur: he tried some of his stale tricks, but soon found that *I* was Yorkshire, too; it would not do—you understand me. We went to the work like good ones, head, heart, and soul; and in fact, since I came here, I have lost no time. I am rather fagged, but I am sure to be well paid for my hardship; I never want sleep so long as I can have the music of a dice-box, and wherewithal to pay the piper. As I told you, he tried some of his queer turns, but I foiled him like a man, and, in return, gave him more than he could relish of the genuine *dead knowledge*. In short, I have plucked the old baronet as never baronet was plucked before; I have scarce left him the stump of a quill. I have got promissory notes in his hand to the amount of—; if you like round numbers, say five-and-twenty thousand pounds, safely

deposited in my portable strong box, alias, double-clasped pocket-book. I leave this ruinous old
rat-hole early on to-morrow, for two reasons: first,
I do not want to play with Sir Arthur deeper than
I think his security would warrant; and, secondly,
because I am safer a hundred miles away from Sir
Arthur than in the house with him. Look you, my
worthy, I tell you this between ourselves—I may
be wrong—but, by—, I am sure as that I am now
living, that Sir A—attempted to poison me last
night. So much for old friendship on both sides.
When I won the last stake, a heavy one enough,
my friend leant his forehead upon his hands, and
you'll laugh when I tell you that his head literally smoked like a hot dumpling. I do not know
whether his agitation was produced by the plan
which he had against me, or by his having lost so
heavily; though it must be allowed that he had
reason to be a little funked, whichever way his
thoughts went; but he pulled the bell, and ordered
two bottles of Champagne. While the fellow was
bringing them, he wrote a promissory note to the
full amount, which he signed, and, as the man
came in with the bottles and glasses, he desired
him to be off. He filled a glass for me, and, while
he thought my eyes were off, for I was putting up
his note at the time, he dropped something slyly
into it, no doubt to sweeten it; but I saw it all, and,
when he handed it to me, I said, with an emphasis

which he might easily understand, 'There is some sediment in it, I'll not drink it.' 'Is there?' said he, and at the same time snatched it from my hand and threw it into the fire. What do you think of that? Have I not a tender bird in hand? Win or lose, I will not play beyond five thousand to-night, and to-morrow sees me safe out of the reach of Sir Arthur's Champagne."

Of the authenticity of this document, I never heard my father express a doubt; and I am satisfied that, owing to his strong conviction in favour of his brother, he would not have admitted it without sufficient inquiry, inasmuch as it tended to confirm the suspicions which already existed to his prejudice. Now, the only point in this letter which made strongly against my uncle, was the mention of the "double-clasped pocket-book," as the receptacle of the papers likely to involve him, for this pocket-book was not forthcoming, nor anywhere to be found, nor had any papers referring to his gaming transactions been discovered upon the dead man.

But whatever might have been the original intention of this man, Collis, neither my uncle nor my father ever heard more of him; he published the letter, however, in Faulkner's newspaper, which was shortly afterwards made the vehicle of a much more mysterious attack. The passage in that journal to which I allude, appeared about four years afterwards, and while the fatal occurrence was still fresh in public recollection. It commenced by a rambling preface, stating that "a *certain person* whom *certain* persons thought to be dead, was not so, but living, and in full possession of his memory, and moreover, ready and able to make *great* delinquents tremble": it then went on to describe the murder, without, however, mentioning names; and in doing so, it entered into minute and circumstantial particulars of which none but an *eye-witness* could have been possessed, and by implications almost too unequivocal to be regarded in the light of insinuation, to involve the "*titled gambler*" in the guilt of the transaction.

My father at once urged Sir Arthur to proceed against the paper in an action of libel, but he would not hear of it, nor consent to my father's taking any legal steps whatever in the matter. My father, however, wrote in a threatening tone to Faulkner, demanding a surrender of the author of the obnoxious article; the answer to this application is still in my possession, and is penned in an apologetic tone: it states that the manuscript had been handed in, paid for, and inserted as an advertisement, without sufficient inquiry, or any knowledge as to whom it referred. No step, however, was taken to clear my uncle's character in the judgment of the public; and, as he immediately sold a small property, the application of the proceeds of which were known to none, he was said to have disposed of it to enable himself to buy off the threatened information; however the truth might have been, it is certain that no charges respecting the mysterious murder were afterwards publicly made against my uncle, and, as far as external disturbances were concerned, he enjoyed henceforward perfect security and quiet.

A deep and lasting impression, however, had been made upon the public mind, and Sir Arthur Tyrrell was no longer visited or noticed by the gentry of the county, whose attentions he had hitherto received. He accordingly affected to despise those courtesies which he no longer enjoyed, and shunned even that society which he might have commanded. This is all that I need recapitulate of my uncle's history, and I now recur to my own.

Although my father had never, within my recollection, visited, or been visited by my uncle, each being of unsocial, procrastinating, and indolent habits, and their respective residences being very far apart—the one lying in the county of Galway, the other in that of Cork—he was strongly attached to his brother, and evinced his affection by an active correspondence, and by deeply and proudly resenting that neglect which had branded Sir Arthur as unfit to mix in society.

When I was about eighteen years of age, my father, whose health had been gradually declining, died, leaving me in heart wretched and desolate, and, owing to his habitual seclusion, with few acquaintances, and almost no friends. The provisions of his will were curious, and when I was sufficiently come to myself to listen to, or comprehend them, surprised me not a little: all his vast property was left to me, and to the heirs of my body, for ever; and, in default of such heirs, it was to go after my death to my uncle, Sir Arthur, without any entail. At the same time, the will appointed him my guardian, desiring that I might be received within his house, and reside with his family, and under his care, during the term of my minority; and in consideration of the increased expense consequent upon such an arrangement, a handsome allowance was allotted to him during the term of my proposed residence. The object of this last provision I at once understood; my father desired, by making it the direct apparent interest of Sir Arthur that I should die without issue, while at the same time he placed my person wholly in his power, to prove to the world how great and unshaken was his confidence in his brother's innocence and honour. It was a strange, perhaps an idle scheme, but as I had been always brought up in the habit of considering my uncle as a deeply injured man, and had been taught, almost as a part of my religion, to regard him as the very soul of honour, I felt no further uneasiness respecting the arrangement than that likely to affect a shy and timid girl at the immediate prospect of taking up her abode for the first time in her life among strangers. Previous to leaving my home, which I felt I should do with a heavy heart, I received a most tender and affectionate letter from my uncle, calculated, if anything could do so, to remove the bitterness of parting from scenes familiar and dear from my earliest childhood, and in some degree to reconcile me to the measure. It was upon a fine autumn day that I approached the old domain of Carrickleigh. I shall not soon forget the impression of sadness and of gloom which all that I saw produced upon my mind; the sunbeams were falling with a rich and melancholy lustre upon the fine old trees, which stood in lordly groups, casting their long sweeping shadows over rock and sward; there was an air of neglect and decay about the spot, which amounted almost to desolation, and mournfully increased as we approached the building itself, near which the ground had been originally more artificially and carefully cultivated than elsewhere, and where consequently neglect more immediately and strikingly betrayed itself.

As we proceeded, the road wound near the beds of what had been formerly two fish-ponds, which were now nothing more than stagnant swamps, overgrown with rank weeds, and here and there encroached upon by the straggling underwood; the avenue itself was much broken; and in many places the stones were almost concealed by grass and nettles; the loose stone walls which had here and there intersected the broad park, were, in many places, broken down, so as no longer to answer their original purpose as fences; piers were now and then to be seen, but the gates were gone; and to add to the general air of dilapidation, some huge trunks were lying scattered through the venerable old trees, either the work of the winter storms, or perhaps the victims of some extensive but desultory scheme of denudation, which the projector had not capital or perseverance to carry into full effect.

After the carriage had travelled a full mile of this avenue, we reached the summit of a rather abrupt eminence, one of the many which added to the picturesqueness, if not to the convenience of this rude approach; from the top of this ridge the grey walls of Carrickleigh were visible, rising at a small distance in front, and darkened by the hoary wood which crowded around them; it was a quadrangular building of considerable extent, and the front, where the great entrance was placed, lay towards us, and bore unequivocal marks of antiquity; the time-worn, solemn aspect of the old building, the ruinous and deserted appearance of the whole place, and the associations which connected it with a dark page in the history of my family, combined to depress spirits already predisposed for the reception of sombre and dejecting impressions. When the carriage drew up in the grass-grown court-yard before the hall-door, two lazy-looking men, whose appearance well accorded with that of the place which they tenanted, alarmed by the obstreperous barking of a great chained dog, ran out from some half-ruinous outhouses, and took charge of the horses; the hall-door stood open, and I entered a gloomy and imperfectly-lighted apartment, and found no one within it. However, I had not long to wait in this awkward predicament, for before my luggage had been deposited in the house, indeed before I had well removed my cloak and other muffles, so as to enable me to look around, a young girl ran lightly into the hall, and kissing me heartily and somewhat boisterously exclaimed, "My dear cousin, my dear Margaret—I am so delighted— so out of breath, we did not expect you till ten o'clock; my father is somewhere about the place, he must be close at hand. James—Corney—run out and tell your master; my brother is seldom at home, at least at any reasonable hour; you must be so tired—so fatigued—let me show you to your room; see that Lady Margaret's luggage is all brought up; you must lie down and rest yourself. Deborah, bring some coffee—up these stairs; we are so delighted to see you—you cannot think how lonely I have been; how steep these stairs are, are not they? I am so glad you are come—I could hardly bring myself to believe that you were really coming; how good of you, dear Lady Margaret." There was real good nature and delight in my cousin's greeting, and a kind of constitutional confidence of manner which placed me at once at ease, and made me feel immediately upon terms of intimacy with her. The room into which she ushered me, although partaking in the general air of decay which pervaded the mansion and all about it, had, nevertheless, been fitted up with evident attention to comfort, and even with some dingy attempt at luxury; but what pleased me most was that it opened, by a second door, upon a lobby which communicated with my fair cousin's apartment; a circumstance which divested the room, in my eyes, of the air of solitude and sadness which would otherwise have characterised it, to a degree almost painful to one so depressed and agitated as I was.

After such arrangements as I found necessary were completed, we both went down to the parlour, a large wainscotted room, hung round with grim old portraits, and, as I was not sorry to see, containing, in its ample grate, a large and cheerful fire. Here my cousin had leisure to talk more at her ease; and from her I learned something of the manners and the habits of the two remaining members of her family, whom I had not yet seen. On my arrival I had known nothing of the family among whom I was come to reside, except that it consisted of three individuals, my uncle, and his son and daughter, Lady Tyrrell having been long dead; in addition to this very scanty stock of information, I shortly learned from my communicative companion, that my uncle was, as I had suspected, completely retired in his habits, and besides that, having been, so far back as she could well recollect, always rather strict, as reformed rakes frequently become, he had latterly been growing more gloomily and sternly religious than heretofore. Her account of her brother was far less favourable, though she did not say anything directly to his disadvantage. From all that I could gather from her, I was led to suppose that he was a specimen of the idle, coarse-mannered, profligate "*squirearchy*"—a result which might naturally have followed from the circumstance of his being, as it were, outlawed from society, and driven for companionship to grades below his own—enjoying, too, the dangerous prerogative of spending a good deal of money. However, you may easily suppose that I found nothing in my cousin's communication fully to bear me out in so very decided a conclusion.

I awaited the arrival of my uncle, which was every moment to be expected, with feelings half of alarm, half of curiosity—a sensation which I have often since experienced, though to a less degree, when upon the point of standing for the first time in the presence of one of whom I have long been in the habit of hearing or thinking with interest. It was, therefore, with some little perturbation that I heard, first a slight bustle at the outer door, then a slow step traverse the hall, and finally witnessed the door open, and my uncle enter the room. He was a striking looking man; from peculiarities both of person and of dress, the whole effect of his appearance amounted to extreme singularity. He was tall, and when young his figure must have been strikingly elegant; as it was, however, its effect was marred by a very decided stoop; his dress was of a sober colour, and in fashion anterior to any thing which I could remember. It was, however, handsome, and by no means carelessly put on; but what completed the singularity of his appearance was his uncut, white hair, which hung in long, but not at all neglected curls, even so far as his shoulders, and which combined with his regularly classic features, and fine dark eyes, to bestow upon him an air of venerable dignity and pride, which I have seldom seen equalled elsewhere. I rose as he entered, and met him about the middle of the room; he kissed my cheek and both my hands, saying—

"You are most welcome, dear child, as welcome as the command of this poor place and all that it contains can make you. I am rejoiced to see you— truly rejoiced. I trust that you are not much fatigued; pray be seated again." He led me to my chair, and continued, "I am glad to perceive you have made acquaintance with Emily already; I see, in your being thus brought together, the foundation of a lasting friendship. You are both innocent, and both young. God bless you—God bless you, and make you all that I could wish."

He raised his eyes, and remained for a few moments silent, as if in secret prayer. I felt that it was impossible that this man, with feelings manifestly so tender, could be the wretch that public opinion had represented him to be. I was more than ever convinced of his innocence. His manners were, or appeared to me, most fascinating. I know not how the lights of experience might have altered this estimate. But I was then very young, and I beheld in him a perfect mingling of the courtesy of polished life with the gentlest and most genial virtues of the heart. A feeling of affection and respect towards him began to spring up within me, the more earnest that I remembered how sorely he had suffered in fortune and how cruelly in fame. My uncle having given me fully to understand that I was most welcome, and might command whatever was his own, pressed me to take some supper; and on my refusing, he observed that, before bidding me good night, he had one duty further to perform, one in which he was convinced I would cheerfully acquiesce. He then proceeded to read from the Bible; after which he took his leave with the same affectionate kindness with which he had greeted me, having repeated his desire that I should consider every thing in his house as altogether at my disposal. It is needless to say how much I was pleased with my uncle—it was impossible to avoid being so; and I could not help saying to myself, if such a man as this is not safe from the assaults of slander, who is? I felt much happier than I had done since my father's death, and enjoyed that night the first refreshing sleep which had visited me since that calamity. My curiosity respecting my male cousin did not long remain unsatisfied; he appeared upon the next day at dinner. His manners, though not so coarse as I had expected, were exceedingly disagreeable; there was an assurance and a forwardness for which I was not prepared; there was less of the vulgarity of manner, and almost more of that of the mind, than I had anticipated. I felt quite uncomfortable in his presence; there was just that confidence in his look and tone, which would read encouragement even in mere toleration; and I felt more disgusted and annoyed at the coarse and extravagant compliments which he was pleased from time to time to pay me, than perhaps the extent of the atrocity might fully have warranted. It was, however, one consolation that he did not often appear, being much engrossed by pursuits about which I neither knew nor cared anything; but when he did, his attentions, either with a view to his amusement, or to some more serious object, were so obviously and perseveringly directed to me, that young and inexperienced as I was, even *I* could not be ignorant of their significance. I felt more provoked by this odious persecution than I can express, and discouraged him with so much vigour, that I did not stop even at rudeness to convince him that his assiduities were unwelcome; but all in vain.

This had gone on for nearly a twelvemonth, to my infinite annoyance, when one day, as I was sitting at some needlework with my companion, Emily, as was my habit, in the parlour, the door opened, and my cousin Edward entered the room. There was something, I thought, odd in his manner, a kind of struggle between shame and impudence, a kind of flurry and ambiguity, which made him appear, if possible, more than ordinarily disagreeable.

"Your servant, ladies," he said, seating himself at the same time; "sorry to spoil your *tete-a-tete*; but never mind, I'll only take Emily's place for a minute or two, and then we part for a while, fair cousin. Emily, my father wants you in the corner turret; no shilly, shally, he's in a hurry." She hesitated. "Be off—tramp, march, I say," he exclaimed, in a tone which the poor girl dared not disobey.

She left the room, and Edward followed her to the door. He stood there for a minute or two, as if reflecting what he should say, perhaps satisfying himself that no one was within hearing in the hall. At length he turned about, having closed the door, as if carelessly, with his foot, and advancing slowly, in deep thought, he took his seat at the side of the table opposite to mine. There was a brief interval of silence, after which he said:—

"I imagine that you have a shrewd suspicion of the object of my early visit; but I suppose I must go into particulars. Must I?"

"I have no conception," I replied, "what your object may be."

"Well, well," said he becoming more at his ease as he proceeded, "it may be told in a few words. You know that it is totally impossible, quite out of the question, that an off-hand young fellow like me, and a good-looking girl like yourself, could meet continually as you and I have done, without an attachment—a liking growing up on one side or other; in short, I think I have let you know as plainly as if I spoke it, that I have been in love with you, almost from the first time I saw you." He paused, but I was too much horrified to speak. He interpreted my silence favourably. "I can tell you," he continued, "I'm reckoned rather hard to please, and very hard to *hit*. I can't say when I was taken with a girl before, so you see fortune reserved me—."

Here the odious wretch actually put his arm round my waist: the action at once restored me to utterance, and with the most indignant vehemence I released myself from his hold, and at the same time said:—

"I *have*, sir, of course, perceived your most disagreeable attentions; they have long been a source
of great annoyance to me; and you must be aware
that I have marked my disapprobation, my dis-
gust, as unequivocally as I possibly could, without
actual indelicacy."

I paused, almost out of breath from the rapidity
with which I had spoken; and without giving him
time to renew the conversation, I hastily quitted
the room, leaving him in a paroxysm of rage and
mortification. As I ascended the stairs, I heard
him open the parlour-door with violence, and
take two or three rapid strides in the direction in
which I was moving. I was now much frightened,
and ran the whole way until I reached my room,
and having locked the door, I listened breathlessly, but heard no sound. This relieved me for the
present; but so much had I been overcome by the
agitation and annoyance attendant upon the scene
which I had just passed through, that when my
cousin Emily knocked at the door, I was weeping
in great agitation. You will readily conceive my
distress, when you reflect upon my strong dislike
to my cousin Edward, combined with my youth
and extreme inexperience. Any proposal of such
a nature must have agitated me; but that it should
come from the man whom, of all others, I instinctively most loathed and abhorred, and to whom I

had, as clearly as manner could do it, expressed the state of my feelings, was almost too annoying to be borne; it was a calamity, too, in which I could not claim the sympathy of my cousin Emily, which had always been extended to me in my minor grievances. Still I hoped that it might not be unattended with good; for I thought that one inevitable and most welcome consequence would result from this painful *eclaircissement*, in the discontinuance of my cousin's odious persecution.

When I arose next morning, it was with the fervent hope that I might never again behold his face, or even hear his name; but such a consummation, though devoutly to be wished, was hardly likely to occur. The painful impressions of yesterday were too vivid to be at once erased; and I could not help feeling some dim foreboding of coming annoyance and evil. To expect on my cousin's part anything like delicacy or consideration for me, was out of the question. I saw that he had set his heart upon my property, and that he was not likely easily to forego such a prize, possessing what might have been considered opportunities and facilities almost to compel my compliance. I now keenly felt the unreasonableness of my father's conduct in placing me to reside with a family, with all the members of which, with one exception, he was wholly unacquainted, and I bitterly felt the helplessness of my situation. I determined, however, in the event of my cousin's persevering in his addresses, to lay all the particulars before my uncle, although he had never, in kindness or intimacy, gone a step beyond our first interview, and to throw myself upon his hospitality and his sense of honour for protection against a repetition of such annoyances.

My cousin's conduct may appear to have been an inadequate cause for such serious uneasiness; but my alarm was awakened neither by his acts nor by words, but entirely by his manner, which was strange and even intimidating. At the beginning of our yesterday's interview, there was a sort of bullying swagger in his air, which, towards the end, gave place to something bordering upon the brutal vehemence of an undisguised ruffian, a transition which had tempted me into a belief that he might seek, even forcibly, to extort from me a consent to his wishes, or by means still more horrible, of which I scarcely dared to trust myself to think, to possess himself of my property.

I was early next day summoned to attend my uncle in his private room, which lay in a corner turret of the old building; and thither I accordingly went, wondering all the way what this unusual measure might prelude. When I entered the room, he did not rise in his usual courteous way to greet me, but simply pointed to a chair opposite to his own; this boded nothing agreeable. I sat down, however, silently waiting until he should open the conversation.

"Lady Margaret," at length he said, in a tone of greater sternness than I thought him capable of using, "I have hitherto spoken to you as a friend, but I have not forgotten that I am also your guardian, and that my authority as such gives me a right to control your conduct. I shall put a question to you, and I expect and will demand a plain, direct answer. Have I rightly been informed that you have contemptuously rejected the suit and hand of my son Edward?"

I stammered forth with a good deal of trepidation:—

"I believe, that is, I have, sir, rejected my cousin's proposals; and my coldness and discouragement might have convinced him that I had determined to do so."

"Madame," replied he, with suppressed, but, as it appeared to me, intense anger, "I have lived long enough to know that *coldness and discouragement*, and such terms, form the common cant of a worthless coquette. You know to the full, as well as I, that *coldness and discouragement* may be so exhibited as to convince their object that he is neither distasteful nor indifferent to the person who wears that manner. You know, too, none better, that an affected neglect, when skillfully managed, is amongst the most formidable of the allurements which artful beauty can employ. I tell you, madame, that having, without one word spoken in discouragement, permitted my son's most marked attentions for a twelvemonth or more, you have no *right* to dismiss him with no further explanation than demurely telling him that you had always looked coldly upon him, and neither your wealth nor *your ladyship* (there was an emphasis of scorn on the word which would have become Sir Giles Overreach himself) can warrant you in treating with contempt the affectionate regard of an honest heart."

I was too much shocked at this undisguised attempt to bully me into an acquiescence in the interested and unprincipled plan for their own aggrandisement, which I now perceived my uncle and his son had deliberately formed, at once to find strength or collectedness to frame an answer to what he had said. At length I replied, with a firmness that surprised myself:—

"In all that you have just now said, sir, you have grossly misstated my conduct and motives. Your information must have been most incorrect, as far as it regards my conduct towards my cousin; my manner towards him could have conveyed nothing but dislike; and if anything could have added to the strong aversion which I have long felt towards him, it would be his attempting thus to frighten me into a marriage which he knows to be revolting to me, and which is sought by him only as a means for securing to himself whatever property is mine."

As I said this, I fixed my eyes upon those of my uncle, but he was too old in the world's ways to falter beneath the gaze of more searching eyes than mine; he simply said—

"Are you acquainted with the provisions of your father's will?"

I answered in the affirmative; and he continued:— "Then you must be aware that if my son Edward were, which God forbid, the unprincipled, reckless man, the ruffian you pretend to think him"— (here he spoke very slowly, as if he intended that every word which escaped him should be registered in my memory, while at the same time the expression of his countenance underwent a gradual but horrible change, and the eyes which he fixed upon me became so darkly vivid, that I almost lost sight of everything else)—"if he were what you have described him, do you think, child, he would have found no shorter way than marriage to gain his ends? A single blow, an outrage not a degree worse than you insinuate, would transfer your property to us!!"

I stood staring at him for many minutes after he had ceased to speak, fascinated by the terrible, serpent-like gaze, until he continued with a welcome change of countenance:—

"I will not speak again to you, upon this topic, until one month has passed. You shall have time to consider the relative advantages of the two courses which are open to you. I should be sorry to hurry you to a decision. I am satisfied with having stated my feelings upon the subject, and pointed out to you the path of duty. Remember this day month; not one word sooner."

He then rose, and I left the room, much agitated and exhausted.

This interview, all the circumstances attending it, but most particularly the formidable expression of my uncle's countenance while he talked, though hypothetically, of *murder*, combined to arouse all my worst suspicions of him. I dreaded to look upon the face that had so recently worn the appalling livery of guilt and malignity. I regarded it with the mingled fear and loathing with which one looks upon an object which has tortured them in a night-mare.

In a few days after the interview, the particulars of which I have just detailed, I found a note upon my toilet-table, and on opening it I read as follows:—

> *"My Dear Lady Margaret,*
>
> You will be, perhaps, surprised to see a strange face in your room today. I have dismissed your Irish maid, and secured a French one to wait upon you; a step rendered necessary by my proposing shortly to visit the Continent with all my family.
>
> Your faithful guardian,
"Arthur Tyrell."

On inquiry, I found that my faithful attendant was actually gone, and far on her way to the town of Galway; and in her stead there appeared a tall, raw-boned, ill-looking, elderly Frenchwoman, whose sullen and presuming manners seemed to imply that her vocation had never before been that of a lady's-maid. I could not help regarding her as a creature of my uncle's, and therefore to be dreaded, even had she been in no other way suspicious.

Days and weeks passed away without any, even a momentary doubt upon my part, as to the course to be pursued by me. The allotted period had at length elapsed; the day arrived upon which I was to communicate my decision to my uncle. Although my resolution had never for a moment wavered, I could not shake off the dread of the approaching colloquy; and my heart sank within me as I heard the expected summons. I had not seen my cousin Edward since the occurrence of the grand *eclair-cissement*; he must have studiously avoided me; I suppose from policy, it could not have been from delicacy. I was prepared for a terrific burst of fury from my uncle, as soon as I should make known my determination; and I not unreasonably feared that some act of violence or of intimidation would next be resorted to. Filled with these dreary forebodings, I fearfully opened the study door, and the next minute I stood in my uncle's presence. He received me with a courtesy which I dreaded, as arguing a favourable anticipation respecting the answer which I was to give; and after some slight delay he began by saying—

"It will be a relief to both of us, I believe, to bring this conversation as soon as possible to an issue. You will excuse me, then, my dear niece, for speaking with a bluntness which, under other circumstances, would be unpardonable. You have, I am certain, given the subject of our last interview fair and serious consideration; and I trust that you are now prepared with candour to lay your answer before me. A few words will suffice; we perfectly understand one another."

He paused; and I, though feeling that I stood upon a mine which might in an instant explode, nevertheless answered with perfect composure: "I must now, sir, make the same reply which I did upon the last occasion, and I reiterate the declaration which I then made, that I never can nor will, while life and reason remain, consent to a union with my cousin Edward."

This announcement wrought no apparent change in Sir Arthur, except that he became deadly, almost lividly pale. He seemed lost in dark thought for a minute, and then, with a slight effort, said, "You have answered me honestly and directly; and you say your resolution is unchangeable; well, would it had been otherwise—would it had been otherwise—but be it as it is; I am satisfied."

He gave me his hand—it was cold and damp as death; under an assumed calmness, it was evident that he was fearfully agitated. He continued to hold my hand with an almost painful pressure, while, as if unconsciously, seeming to forget my presence, he muttered, "Strange, strange, strange, indeed! fatuity, helpless fatuity!" there was here a long pause. "Madness *indeed* to strain a cable that is rotten to the very heart; it must break— and then—all goes." There was again a pause of some minutes, after which, suddenly changing his voice and manner to one of wakeful alacrity, he exclaimed,

"Margaret, my son Edward shall plague you no more. He leaves this country to-morrow for France; he shall speak no more upon this subject—never, never more; whatever events depended upon your answer must now take their own course; but as for this fruitless proposal, it has been tried enough; it can be repeated no more."

At these words he coldly suffered my hand to drop, as if to express his total abandonment of all his projected schemes of alliance; and certainly the action, with the accompanying words, produced upon my mind a more solemn and depressing effect than I believed possible to have been caused by the course which I had determined to pursue; it struck upon my heart with an awe and heaviness which *will* accompany the accomplishment of an important and irrevocable act, even though no doubt or scruple remains to make it possible that the agent should wish it undone.

"Well," said my uncle, after a little time, "we now cease to speak upon this topic, never to resume it again. Remember you shall have no farther uneasiness from Edward; he leaves Ireland for France to-morrow; this will be a relief to you; may I depend upon your *honour* that no word touching the subject of this interview shall ever escape you?" I gave him the desired assurance; he said, "It is well; I am satisfied; we have nothing more, I believe, to say upon either side, and my presence must be a restraint upon you, I shall therefore bid you farewell." I then left the apartment, scarcely knowing what to think of the strange interview which had just taken place.

On the next day my uncle took occasion to tell me that Edward had actually sailed, if his intention had not been prevented by adverse winds or weather; and two days after he actually produced a letter from his son, written, as it said, *on board*, and despatched while the ship was getting under weigh. This was a great satisfaction to me, and as being likely to prove so, it was no doubt communicated to me by Sir Arthur.

During all this trying period I had found infinite consolation in the society and sympathy of my dear cousin Emily. I never, in after-life, formed a friendship so close, so fervent, and upon which,

in all its progress, I could look back with feelings of such unalloyed pleasure, upon whose termination I must ever dwell with so deep, so yet
unembittered a sorrow. In cheerful converse with
her I soon recovered my spirits considerably, and
passed my time agreeably enough, although still
in the utmost seclusion. Matters went on smoothly enough, although I could not help sometimes
feeling a momentary, but horrible uncertainty respecting my uncle's character; which was not altogether unwarranted by the circumstances of the
two trying interviews, the particulars of which
I have just detailed. The unpleasant impression
which these conferences were calculated to leave
upon my mind was fast wearing away, when
there occurred a circumstance, slight indeed in
itself, but calculated irrepressibly to awaken all
my worst suspicions, and to overwhelm me again
with anxiety and terror.

I had one day left the house with my cousin
Emily, in order to take a ramble of considerable
length, for the purpose of sketching some favourite views, and we had walked about half a mile
when I perceived that we had forgotten our drawing materials, the absence of which would have
defeated the object of our walk. Laughing at our
own thoughtlessness, we returned to the house,
and leaving Emily outside, I ran upstairs to

procure the drawing-books and pencils which lay in my bed-room. As I ran up the stairs, I was met by the tall, ill-looking Frenchwoman, evidently a good deal flurried; "Que veut Madame?" said she, with a more decided effort to be polite, than I had ever known her make before. "No, no—no matter," said I, hastily running by her in the direction of my room. "Madame," cried she, in a high key, "restez ici s'il vous plait, votre chambre n'est pas faite." I continued to move on without heeding her. She was some way behind me, and feeling that she could not otherwise prevent my entrance, for I was now upon the very lobby, she made a desperate attempt to seize hold of my person; she succeeded in grasping the end of my shawl, which she drew from my shoulders, but slipping at the same time upon the polished oak floor, she fell at full length upon the boards. A little frightened as well as angry at the rudeness of this strange woman, I hastily pushed open the door of my room, at which I now stood, in order to escape from her; but great was my amazement on entering to find the apartment preoccupied. The window was open, and beside it stood two male figures; they appeared to be examining the fastenings of the casement, and their backs were turned towards the door. One of them was my uncle; they both had turned on my entrance, as if startled; the stranger was booted and cloaked, and wore a heavy, broad-leafed hat over his brows; he turned but for a moment, and averted his face; but I had seen enough to convince me that he was no other than my cousin Edward. My uncle had some iron instrument in his hand, which he hastily concealed behind his back; and coming towards me, said something as if in an explanatory tone; but I was too much shocked and confounded to understand what it might be. He said something about "*repairs*—window-frames—cold, and safety." I did not wait, however, to ask or to receive explanations, but hastily left the room. As I went down stairs I thought I heard the voice of the Frenchwoman in all the shrill volubility of excuse, and others uttering suppressed but vehement imprecations, or what seemed to me to be such.

I joined my cousin Emily quite out of breath. I need not say that my head was too full of other things to think much of drawing for that day. I imparted to her frankly the cause of my alarms, but, at the same time, as gently as I could; and with tears she promised vigilance, devotion, and love. I never had reason for a moment to repent the unreserved confidence which I then reposed in her. She was no less surprised than I at the unexpected appearance of Edward, whose departure for France neither of us had for a moment doubted, but which was now proved by his actual presence to be nothing more than an imposture practised, I feared, for no good end. The situation in which I had found my uncle had very nearly removed all my doubts as to his designs; I magnified suspicions into certainties, and dreaded night after night that I should be murdered in my bed. The nervousness produced by sleepless nights and days of anxious fears increased the horrors of my situation to such a degree, that I at length wrote a letter to a Mr. Jefferies, an old and faithful friend of my father's, and perfectly acquainted with all his affairs, praying him, for God's sake, to relieve me from my present terrible situation, and communicating without reserve the nature and grounds of my suspicions. This letter I kept sealed and directed for two or three days always about my person, for discovery would have been ruinous, in expectation of an opportunity, which might be safely trusted, of having it placed in the post-office; as neither Emily nor I were permitted to pass beyond the precincts of the demesne itself, which was surrounded by high walls formed of dry stone, the difficulty of procuring such an opportunity was greatly enhanced.

At this time Emily had a short conversation with her father, which she reported to me instantly. After some indifferent matter, he had asked her whether she and I were upon good terms, and whether I was unreserved in my disposition. She answered in the affirmative; and he then inquired whether I had been much surprised to find him in my chamber on the other day. She answered that I had been both surprised and amused. "And what did she think of George Wilson's appearance?" "Who?" inquired she. "Oh! the architect," he answered, "who is to contract for the repairs of the house; he is accounted a handsome fellow." "She could not see his face," said Emily, "and she was in such a hurry to escape that she scarcely observed him." Sir Arthur appeared satisfied, and the conversation ended.

This slight conversation, repeated accurately to me by Emily, had the effect of confirming, if indeed any thing was required to do so, all that I had before believed as to Edward's actual presence; and I naturally became, if possible, more anxious than ever to despatch the letter to Mr. Jefferies. An opportunity at length occurred. As Emily and I were walking one day near the gate of the demesne, a lad from the village happened to be passing down the avenue from the house; the spot was secluded, and as this person was not connected by service with those whose observation I dreaded, I committed the letter to his keeping, with strict injunctions that he should put it, without delay, into the receiver of the town post-office; at the same time I added a suitable gratuity, and the man having made many protestations of punctuality, was soon out of sight. He was hardly gone when I began to doubt my discretion in having trusted him; but I had no better or safer means of despatching the letter, and I was not warranted in suspecting him of such wanton dishonesty as a disposition to tamper with it; but I could not be quite satisfied of its safety until I had received an answer, which could not arrive for a few days. Before I did, however, an event occurred which a little surprised me. I was sitting in my bed-room early in the day, reading by myself, when I heard a knock at the door. "Come in," said I, and my uncle entered the room. "Will you excuse me," said he, "I sought you in the parlour, and thence I have come here. I desired to say a word to you. I trust that you have hitherto found my conduct to you such as that of a guardian towards his ward should be." I dared not withhold my assent. "And," he continued, "I trust that you have not found me harsh or unjust, and that you have perceived, my dear niece, that I have sought to make this poor place as agreeable to you as may be?" I assented again; and he put his hand in his pocket, whence he drew a folded paper, and dashing it upon the table with startling emphasis he said, "Did you write that letter?" The sudden and fearful alteration of his voice, manner, and face, but more than all, the unexpected production of my letter to Mr. Jefferies, which I at once recognised, so confounded and terrified me, that I felt almost choking. I could not utter a word. "Did you write that letter?" he repeated, with slow and intense emphasis. "You did, liar and hypocrite. You dared to write that foul and infamous libel; but it shall be your last. Men will universally believe you mad, if I choose to call for an inquiry. I can make you appear so. The suspicions expressed in this letter are the hallucinations and alarms of a moping lunatic. I have defeated your first attempt, madam; and by the holy God, if ever you make another, chains, darkness, and the keeper's whip shall be your portion." With these astounding words he left the room, leaving me almost fainting.

I was now almost reduced to despair; my last cast had failed; I had no course left but that of escaping secretly from the castle, and placing myself under the protection of the nearest magistrate. I felt if this were not done, and speedily, that I should be *murdered*. No one, from mere description, can have an idea of the unmitigated horror of my situation; a helpless, weak, inexperienced girl, placed under the power, and wholly at the mercy of evil men, and feeling that I had it not in my power to escape for one moment from the malignant influences under which I was probably doomed to fall; with a consciousness, too, that if violence, if murder were designed, no human being would be near to aid me; my dying shriek would be lost in void space.

I had seen Edward but once during his visit, and as I did not meet him again, I began to think that he must have taken his departure; a conviction which was to a certain degree satisfactory, as I regarded his absence as indicating the removal of immediate danger. Emily also arrived circuitously at the same conclusion, and not without good grounds, for she managed indirectly to learn that Edward's black horse had actually been for a day and part of a night in the castle stables, just at the time of her brother's supposed visit. The horse had gone, and as she argued, the rider must have departed with it.

This point being so far settled, I felt a little less uncomfortable; when being one day alone in my bed-room, I happened to look out from the window, and to my unutterable horror, I beheld peering through an opposite casement, my cousin Edward's face. Had I seen the evil one himself in bodily shape, I could not have experienced a more sickening revulsion. I was too much appalled to move at once from the window, but I did so soon enough to avoid his eye. He was looking fixedly down into the narrow quadrangle upon which the window opened. I shrunk back unperceived, to pass the rest of the day in terror and despair. I went to my room early that night, but I was too miserable to sleep.

At about twelve o'clock, feeling very nervous, I determined to call my cousin Emily, who slept, you will remember, in the next room, which communicated with mine by a second door. By this private entrance I found my way into her chamber, and without difficulty persuaded her to return to my room and sleep with me. We accordingly lay down together, she undressed, and I with my clothes on, for I was every moment walking up and down the room, and felt too nervous and miserable to think of rest or comfort. Emily was soon fast asleep, and I lay awake, fervently longing for the first pale gleam of morning, and reckoning every stroke of the old clock with an impatience which made every hour appear like six.

It must have been about one o'clock when I thought I heard a slight noise at the partition door between Emily's room and mine, as if caused by somebody's turning the key in the lock. I held my breath, and the same sound was repeated at the second door of my room, that which opened upon the lobby; the sound was here distinctly caused by the revolution of the bolt in the lock, and it was followed by a slight pressure upon the door itself, as if to ascertain the security of the lock. The person, whoever it might be, was probably satisfied, for I heard the old boards of the lobby creak and strain, as if under the weight of somebody moving cautiously over them. My sense of hearing became unnaturally, almost painfully acute. I suppose the imagination added distinctness to sounds vague in themselves. I thought that I could actually hear the breathing of the person who was slowly returning along the lobby.

At the head of the stair-case there appeared to occur a pause; and I could distinctly hear two or three sentences hastily whispered; the steps then descended the stairs with apparently less caution. I ventured to walk quickly and lightly to the lobby door, and attempted to open it; it was indeed fast locked upon the outside, as was also the other. I now felt that the dreadful hour was come; but one desperate expedient remained—it was to awaken Emily, and by our united strength, to attempt to force the partition door, which was slighter than the other, and through this to pass to the lower part of the house, whence it might be possible to escape to the grounds, and so to the village. I returned to the bedside, and shook Emily, but in vain; nothing that I could do availed to produce from her more than a few incoherent words; it was a death-like sleep. She had certainly drunk of some narcotic, as, probably, had I also, in spite of all the caution with which I had examined every thing presented to us to eat or drink. I now attempted, with as little noise as possible, to force first one door, then the other; but all in vain. I believe no strength could have affected my object, for both doors opened inwards. I therefore collected whatever moveables I could carry thither, and piled them against the doors, so as to assist me in whatever attempts I should make to resist the entrance of those without. I then returned to the bed and endeavoured again, but fruitlessly, to awaken my cousin. It was not sleep, it was torpor, lethargy, death. I knelt down and prayed with an agony of earnestness; and then seating myself upon the bed, I awaited my fate with a kind of terrible tranquillity.

I heard a faint clanking sound from the narrow court which I have already mentioned, as if caused by the scraping of some iron instrument against stones or rubbish. I at first determined not to disturb the calmness which I now experienced, by uselessly watching the proceedings of those who sought my life; but as the sounds continued, the horrible curiosity which I felt overcame every other emotion, and I determined, at all hazards, to gratify it. I, therefore, crawled upon my knees to the window, so as to let the smallest possible portion of my head appear above the sill.

The moon was shining with an uncertain radiance upon the antique grey buildings, and obliquely upon the narrow court beneath; one side of it was therefore clearly illuminated, while the other was lost in obscurity, the sharp outlines of the old gables, with their nodding clusters of ivy, being at first alone visible. Whoever or whatever occasioned the noise which had excited my curiosity, was concealed under the shadow of the dark side of the quadrangle. I placed my hand over my eyes to shade them from the moonlight, which was so bright as to be almost dazzling, and, peering into the darkness, I first dimly, but afterwards gradually, almost with full distinctness, beheld the form of a man engaged in digging what appeared to be a rude hole close under the wall. Some implements, probably a shovel and pickaxe, lay beside him, and to these he every now and then applied himself as the nature of the ground required. He pursued his task rapidly, and with as little noise as possible. "So," thought I, as shovelful after shovelful, the dislodged rubbish mounted into a heap, "they are digging the grave in which, before two hours pass, I must lie, a cold, mangled corpse. I am *theirs*—I cannot escape." I felt as if my reason was leaving me. I started to my feet, and in mere despair I applied myself again to each of the two doors alternately. I strained every nerve and sinew, but I might as well have attempted, with my single strength, to force the building itself from its foundations. I threw myself madly upon the ground, and clasped my hands over my eyes as if to shut out the horrible images which crowded upon me.

The paroxysm passed away. I prayed once more with the bitter, agonised fervour of one who feels that the hour of death is present and inevitable. When I arose, I went once more to the window and looked out, just in time to see a shadowy figure glide stealthily along the wall. The task was finished. The catastrophe of the tragedy must soon be accomplished. I determined now to defend my life to the last; and that I might be able to do so with some effect, I searched the room for something which might serve as a weapon; but either through accident, or else in anticipation of such a possibility, every thing which might have been made available for such a purpose had been removed.

I must then die tamely and without an effort to defend myself. A thought suddenly struck me; might it not be possible to escape through the door, which the assassin must open in order to enter the room? I resolved to make the attempt. I felt assured that the door through which ingress to the room would be effected was that which opened upon the lobby. It was the more direct way, besides being, for obvious reasons, less liable to interruption than the other. I resolved, then, to place myself behind a projection of the wall, the shadow would serve fully to conceal me, and when the door should be opened, and before they should have discovered the identity of the occupant of the bed, to creep noiselessly from the room, and then to trust to Providence for escape. In order to facilitate this scheme, I removed all the lumber which I had heaped against the door; and I had nearly completed my arrangements, when I perceived the room suddenly darkened, by the close approach of some shadowy object to the window. On turning my eyes in that direction, I observed at the top of the casement, as if suspended from above, first the feet, then the legs, then the body, and at length the whole figure of a man present itself. It was Edward Tyrrell. He appeared to be guiding his descent so as to bring his feet upon the centre of the stone block which occupied the lower part of the window; and having secured his footing upon this, he kneeled down and began to gaze into the room. As the moon was gleaming into the chamber, and the bed-curtains were drawn, he was able to distinguish the bed itself and its contents. He appeared satisfied with his scrutiny, for he looked up and made a sign with his hand. He then applied his hands to the window-frame, which must have been ingeniously contrived for the purpose, for with apparently no resistance the whole frame, containing casement and all, slipped from its position in the wall, and was by him lowered into the room. The cold night wind waved the bed-curtains, and he paused for a moment; all was still again, and he stepped in upon the floor of the room. He held in his hand what appeared to be a steel instrument, shaped something like a long hammer. This he held rather behind him, while, with three long, *tip-toe* strides, he brought himself to the bedside. I felt that the discovery must now be made, and held my breath in momentary expectation of the execration in which he would vent his surprise and disappointment. I closed my eyes; there was a pause, but it was a short one. I heard two dull blows, given in rapid succession; a quivering sigh, and the long-drawn, heavy breathing of the sleeper was for ever suspended. I unclosed my eyes, and saw the murderer fling the quilt across the head of his victim; he then, with the instrument of death still in his hand, proceeded to the lobby-door, upon which he tapped sharply twice or thrice. A quick step was then heard approaching, and a voice whispered something from without. Edward answered, with a kind of shuddering chuckle, "Her ladyship is past complaining; unlock the door, in the devil's name, unless you're afraid to come in, and help me to lift her out of the window." The key was turned in the lock, the door opened, and my uncle entered the room. I have told you already that I had placed myself under the shade of a projection of the wall, close to the door. I had instinctively shrunk down cowering towards the ground on the entrance of Edward through the window. When my uncle entered the room, he and his son both stood so very close to me that his hand was every moment upon the point of touching my face. I held my breath, and remained motionless as death.

"You had no interruption from the next room?" said my uncle.

"No," was the brief reply.

"Secure the jewels, Ned; the French harpy must not lay her claws upon them. You're a steady hand, by G—d; not much blood—eh?"

"Not twenty drops," replied his son, "and those on the quilt."

"I'm glad it's over," whispered my uncle again; "we must lift the—the *thing* through the window, and lay the rubbish over it."

They then turned to the bedside, and, winding the bed-clothes round the body, carried it between them slowly to the window, and exchanging a few brief words with some one below, they shoved it over the window-sill, and I heard it fall heavily on the ground underneath.

"I'll take the jewels," said my uncle; "there are two caskets in the lower drawer."

He proceeded, with an accuracy which, had I been more at ease, would have furnished me with matter of astonishment, to lay his hand upon the very spot where my jewels lay; and having possessed himself of them, he called to his son:—

"Is the rope made fast above?"

"I'm no fool; to be sure it is," replied he.

They then lowered themselves from the window; and I rose lightly and cautiously, scarcely daring to breathe, from my place of concealment, and was creeping towards the door, when I heard my uncle's voice, in a sharp whisper, exclaim, "Get up again; G—d d—n you, you've forgot to lock the room door"; and I perceived, by the straining of the rope which hung from above, that the mandate was instantly obeyed. Not a second was to be lost. I passed through the door, which was only closed, and moved as rapidly as I could, consistently with stillness, along the lobby. Before I had gone many yards, I heard the door through which I had just passed roughly locked on the inside. I glided down the stairs in terror, lest, at every corner, I should meet the murderer or one of his accomplices. I reached the hall, and listened, for a moment, to ascertain whether all was silent around. No sound was audible; the parlour windows opened on the park, and through one of them I might, I thought, easily effect my escape. Accordingly, I hastily entered; but, to my consternation, a candle was burning in the room, and by its light I saw a figure seated at the dinner-table, upon which lay glasses, bottles, and the other accompaniments of a drinking party. Two or three chairs were placed about the table, irregularly, as if hastily abandoned by their occupants. A single glance satisfied me that the figure was that of my French attendant. She was fast asleep, having, probably, drank deeply. There was something malignant and ghastly in the calmness of this bad woman's features, dimly illuminated as they were by the flickering blaze of the candle. A knife lay upon the table, and the terrible thought struck me—"Should I kill this sleeping accomplice in the guilt of the murderer, and thus secure my retreat?" Nothing could be easier; it was but to draw the blade across her throat, the work of a second.

An instant's pause, however, corrected me. "No," thought I, "the God who has conducted me thus far through the valley of the shadow of death, will not abandon me now. I will fall into their hands, or I will escape hence, but it shall be free from the stain of blood; His will be done." I felt a confidence arising from this reflection, an assurance of protection which I cannot describe. There were no other means of escape, so I advanced, with a firm step and collected mind, to the window. I noiselessly withdrew the bars, and unclosed the shutters; I pushed open the casement, and without waiting to look behind me, I ran with my utmost speed, scarcely feeling the ground beneath me, down the avenue, taking care to keep upon the grass which bordered it. I did not for a moment slacken my speed, and I had now gained the central point between the park-gate and the mansion-house. Here the avenue made a wider circuit, and in order to avoid delay, I directed my way across the smooth sward round which the carriageway wound, intending, at the opposite side of the level, at a point which I distinguished by a group of old birch trees, to enter again upon the beaten track, which was from thence tolerably direct to the gate. I had, with my utmost speed, got about half way across this broad flat, when the rapid tramp of a horse's hoofs struck upon my ear. My heart swelled in my bosom, as though I would smother. The clattering of galloping hoofs approached; I was pursued; they were now upon the sward on which I was running; there was not a bush or a bramble to shelter me; and, as if to render escape altogether desperate, the moon, which had hitherto been obscured, at this moment shone forth with a broad, clear light, which made every object distinctly visible. The sounds were now close behind me. I felt my knees bending under me, with the sensation which unnerves one in a dream. I reeled, I stumbled, I fell; and at the same instant the cause of my alarm wheeled past me at full gallop. It was one of the young fillies which pastured loose about the park, whose frolics had thus all but maddened me with terror. I scrambled to my feet, and rushed on with weak but rapid steps, my sportive companion still galloping round and round me with many a frisk and fling, until, at length, more dead than alive, I reached the avenue-gate, and crossed the stile, I scarce knew how. I ran through the village, in which all was silent as the grave, until my progress was arrested by the hoarse voice of a sentinel, who cried "Who goes there?" I felt that I was now safe. I turned in the direction of the voice, and fell fainting at the soldier's feet. When I came to myself, I was sitting in a miserable hovel, surrounded by strange faces, all bespeaking curiosity and compassion. Many soldiers were in it also; indeed, as I afterwards found, it was employed as a guard-room by a detachment of troops quartered for that night in the town. In a few words I informed their officer of the circumstances which had occurred, describing also the appearance of the persons engaged in the murder; and he, without further loss of time than was necessary to procure the attendance of a magistrate, proceeded to the mansion-house of Carrickleigh, taking with him a party of his men. But the villains had discovered their mistake, and had effected their escape before the arrival of the military.

The Frenchwoman was, however, arrested in the neighbourhood upon the next day. She was tried and condemned at the ensuing assizes; and previous to her execution confessed that "*she had a hand in making Hugh Tisdall's bed.*" She had been a housekeeper in the castle at the time, and a *chere amie* of my uncle's. She was, in reality, able to speak English like a native, but had exclusively used the French language, I suppose to facilitate her designs. She died the same hardened wretch she had lived, confessing her crimes only, as she alleged, that her doing so might involve Sir Arthur Tyrrell, the great author of her guilt and misery, and whom she now regarded with unmitigated detestation.

With the particulars of Sir Arthur's and his son's escape, as far as they are known, you are acquainted. You are also in possession of their after fate; the terrible, the tremendous retribution which, after long delays of many years, finally overtook and crushed them. Wonderful and inscrutable are the dealings of God with his creatures!

Deep and fervent as must always be my gratitude to heaven for my deliverance, effected by a chain of providential occurrences, the failing of a single link of which must have ensured my destruction, it was long before I could look back upon it with other feelings than those of bitterness, almost of agony. The only being that had ever really loved me, my nearest and dearest friend, ever ready to sympathise, to counsel, and to assist; the gayest, the gentlest, the warmest heart; the only creature on earth that cared for me; *her* life had been the price of my deliverance; and I then uttered the wish, which no event of my long and sorrowful life has taught me to recall, that she had been spared, and that, in her stead, *I* were mouldering in the grave, forgotten, and at rest.